William Forsyth

Idylls and Lyrics

William Forsyth

Idylls and Lyrics

ISBN/EAN: 9783744769211

Printed in Europe, USA, Canada, Australia, Japan

Cover: Foto ©Andreas Hilbeck / pixelio.de

More available books at **www.hansebooks.com**

IDYLLS AND LYRICS

BY

WILLIAM FORSYTH

AUTHOR OF 'KELAVANE,' ETC.

> " I sat me down to watch upon a bank
> With ivy canopied, and interwove
> With flaunting honeysuckle, and began,
> Wrapt in a pleasing fit of melancholy,
> To meditate my rural minstrelsy,
> Till fancy had her fill."
> —MILTON's *Comus*.

WILLIAM BLACKWOOD AND SONS
EDINBURGH AND LONDON
MDCCCLXXII

MANY of these Poems were written long ago, and appeared in one or other of the principal periodicals of the day, including 'Blackwood's Magazine,' 'Punch,' 'The Cornhill Magazine,' 'The Dublin University Magazine,' and 'Good Words.'

CONTENTS.

249

III. NOW AND THEN—

I.

FAMILIAR THINGS

" Ex noto fictum carmen sequar, ut sibi quivis
Speret idem."
—HORACE.

I would choose some familiar subject for a poem, and treat it in a simple way, so that any one might think he could do the same. —*Free Translation.*

THE OLD KIRK BELL.

I.

THEY sing the lays
Of golden days,
But sweetest tongue could never
Tell half the bliss
Of a day like this,
Although it sung For ever.
The green earth breathes its hymns of praise,
And fragrance through the air ;
And the day is as fair as the golden days,
Of the times that never were.

II.

A day all light,
All song, all rest,
With sunshine brightly glowing !
A cup divine
Of amethyst
With golden wine o'erflowing !
The far-off hills, half-brown, half-blue,
The far-off sea of silver rays,
The woodland homes that glimmer through
The faint sweet gleams of summer haze !

III.

A day of rest,
Of light and song,
A perfect thing and peerless,
When life is blest
And love is strong,
And timid things are fearless;
And one sweet sound runs through it all,
Through hearts and homes, o'er hills and dells,
Through all the land with kindly call,
The faint and far-off sound of bells.

IV.

It wakes one thought,
It makes one mind,
One kindred lot and common feeling,
One truth to tell,
One tie to bind,
Where that old bell is pealing.
It comes the echo of a sound,
All faint and fitful through the wood;
It trembles o'er the meadow-ground,
And wakes the moorland solitude.

V.

They said old bells
Were saintly bells,
Made so by rites baptismal,
And every shade
Unhallowèd,
And sounds and sights all dread and dismal,
At their sweet swell fled far away,
And left the earth to better things;
And is it so, on this clear day,
When the grey old kirk bell rings?

VI.

Not as they tell
With mystic sound
Their virtue round us flinging,
When every hour,
From its grey tower,
Some convent bell was ringing.
These times have still the mellow glow
That many a rare old picture wears:
But lights and shadows come and go;
The spirit lives through all the years.

VII.

And when I hear
The old kirk bell
Ring clearly near, or far and faintly,
Loud on the hill,
Low in the dell,
I deem it still half saintly.
But less for rites, or old or new,
Than for one long perpetual call
To be of faithful heart and true;
One truth to you, to me, to all.

VIII.

It rings upon
The good plough-lands
The weary hands to waken ;
It rings to bless
The wilderness
By love still unforsaken.
To old and young, to rich and poor,
To those who go, and those who wait,
It rings in at the cottage door,
And at the castle gate.

IX.

Ring out, sweet bell !
The cock's shrill crow
Is answered well and widely ;
The watch-dog's bay
At close of day
Is answered, though but idly.
But o'er the land, and through the land,
Ten thousand bells responsive ring ;
And when they cease, sweet hymns of peace,
The myriad voices sing.

X.

By peaceful town
Whose sons of toil
The bells ring down the alleys ;
By fields where rest
Both man and beast
Amid the silent valleys ;
By still white farms, and quiet ways,
And lands all clothed with kine and corn,—
With something of Saturnian days,
Comes down the golden Sabbath morn.

XI.

The tremulous air
Seems hushed with prayer,
With summer balm is laden ;
While through the calm
Come hymns that seem
A far-off dream of Eden.
I know not whence or how they come,
The white-robed thoughts of better times,
But that old Mammon's rites are dumb
Before the saintly Sabbath chimes.

XII.

The purple light
Of Palestine
Not faded quite, nor fading,
Its ancient ray,
Its sacred sign,
On this one day is shedding.
The fallow of the weary ground,
The hour of nature's jubilee,
The day, when every brow is crowned,
And every hand is free.

XIII.

This old kirk-road
Our fathers trod,—
Have trod through ages olden,
By grassy ways,
And broomy braes,
And whinny hedges golden.
Both young and old, they've come and gone,
At the kirk bell's kindly call;
They've left their footprints on the stone,
Their shadows on the wall.

XIV.

And still and well
The old kirk bell
Rings out, to tell us ever
The truth it told
The men of old,
Ere it tolled them o'er the river.
The sweet old bell that rang them home—
The faithful hearts that throb no more—
Will welcome in the years to come,
Will toll them down the silent shore.

XV.

It brings with it
Old memories,
Old presences, old voices,
Like some sweet song
Remembered long,
That saddens, yet rejoices.
God's acre bears a greener sward
As we grow old, and live to say,—
I have more friends in yon kirkyard
Than in the whole wide world this day.

XVI.

I would recite
` The words of one
Who held supernal light delusion ;
Who thought, resolved,
Believed, alone,
In his own self-evolved conclusion.
Whate'er the change wrought change on him,
In weary years and far-off climes,
Through dreams and doubts all dusky dim
Come some faint lights from better times :—

XVII.

Could I but hear
The old kirk bell—
And it rings well and clearly ;
Could I but see
The faces dear
Still loved by me so dearly;
It would bring me back my mother's voice,
And the home-light of her face,
And make my heart once more rejoice
With all its early tenderness.

XVIII.

Could I but hear
The voices clear
That sung the good Old Hundred—
Its tones so sweet
Again to greet
At home among my kindred;
I think I would feel as once I felt,
And sing as once I sung;
I think I would kneel as once I knelt
In the days when I was young.

XIX.

The simple calm !
The sacred rest !
The open-handed meeting,
When labour's palm
Is only pressed
By kindly neighbours greeting !
I mind the preacher's reverend air,
Each elder's grave and kindly face—
The dewy eyes that lingered where
Some dear one had his resting-place.

XX.

And could I hear
The old kirk bell
Among the dear old mountains,
I sometimes feel
The silent well
Might still unseal its fountains.
They say that long-polluted springs
Forsake their founts and cease to flow ;
But something more than memory brings
Those sad sweet thoughts of long ago.

XXI.

It was no weak
Heart's sick-bed thought,
Forgot, when sick no longer ;
His footstep sought
His home anew,
As home-love grew the stronger.
The old bell rang his welcome home,
In waves of sound that beat the shore
From unseen lands, from whence have come
The tidings of the Evermore.

XXII.

Not as of old,
With mystic sound,
Its virtue round him flinging;
The bells of gold
That Aaron wore
He knew no more were ringing,
Than were the bells of Babylon,
Or where Osiris' worship sprang,
Or where around Cybele's throne
Her Corybantes cymbals rang.

XXIII.

Before the light
The symbols pale
That form and rite portended;
The Temple veil
Is rent in twain,
The reign of shadows ended;
Yet while I know the silent gaze
Of some who fix their eyes above,
I likewise know the thousand ways
That others take to tell their love.

XXIV.

I daresay each
Hath rites and runes   .
He doth not teach—all moving,
To sweet old tunes
That come and go,   .
Yet merit no reproving.
The buried years, they are not dead
To memory fraught with treasure-trove,—
The gems that have their lustre shed
O'er hero life, and homely love.

XXV.

But men who piled
Their arms to pray,
While wife and child they guarded,
And held the faith
In battle-day,
By life or death rewarded,
A grandly simple creed had they—
The soul's dominion broad and free,
Where priest and king with royal sway
Each man by Christ's dear blood should be.

XXVI.

The heather moor
Was their kirk floor,
Its roof the cloud of heaven ;
It heard their songs,
It drank their blood,
It saw their wrongs forgiven.
As little recked they where they knelt,
As when for truth they fought or fell.
By their brave deeds their church they built ;
They gave their blood to build it well.

XXVII.

On God's own hill
It was the still
Small voice, and not the thunder.
The tempest dire,
Earthquake and fire,
The great rocks smote asunder,
But God was not in these—the wind,
The earthquake, or the flame—
But in the Still Small Voice behind,
That to the Tishbite came.

XXVIII.

For form and rite
Symbolical
From Horeb's height of glory
Come, blended with
Full many a myth,
The light of Pagan story.
Still to illuminate the Word
With earth-born rays men's hearts rejoice ;
But aye for us the present Lord
Is in the Still Small Voice.

XXIX.

And far upon
The misty hill,
And on the lonely ocean,
And on the still
Dread desert sands,
And 'mid the land's devotion,
The word goes forth, the same—the same—
Alike, though strange and homely things,
Not more in earthquake or in flame
Than in the song the linnet sings.

B

XXX.

What though the power
That ruleth o'er
The heart of things be hidden?
And what, and whence,
The influence,
When beauty springs unbidden?
And what the law and what the force—
The same all time and nature through—
That bind the planets in their course,
And mould the drops of morning dew?

XXXI.

Though closed the reign
Of symbols now,
We break no chain asunder,
That links our time
Through days sublime
With Horeb's brow of thunder.
They shone amid the altar flame,
They saw the last dread victim fall,
When through the Gates of Glory came
The Lord of Love that changed them all.

XXXII.

The old, the new,
The ever true,
All nature through have bound us
With cords first wove
Of law, then love,
And wound all round and round us.
They bind us like the starry host
That in their stately order shine :
No star is dark, no word is lost,
But Love hath made them all divine.

XXXIII.

The heart alone
God's temple is,
And there His throne and altar ;
The sacrifice
Is there, the priest,
The fast, the feast, the psalter.
There, too, doth reign the Paraclete ;
And like a star the soul doth move
In its great orbit firmly set,
If sphered by Truth and ruled by Love.

XXXIV.

As star to star,
So man to man;
Though thither far, and hither,
Their footsteps fall,
One boundless plan
Doth bind them all together.
And one great action centres time;
One thought a thousand bosoms feel,
And feel the more, make more sublime
The wider their divine appeal.

XXXV.

But what am I
To sit and sing
Lone on a hill,—half dreaming
Of many a high
And holy thing,
That may be still but seeming,
To one apart from all this strong,
Deep theme of life, and purpose calm,
That make as one that mighty throng,
As one their many-voicèd psalm?

XXXVI.

Yet when I hear
The old kirk bell
Ring clearly near, or far and faintly,
Loud on the hill,
Low in the dell,
I deem it still half saintly.
Whate'er the rite, the prayer, the praise,
The immemorial Record tells
Of Time's long chain of Sabbath-days
Like resting-spots by desert wells.

XXXVII.

The days of rest
From age to age,
A chain of gold unbroken !
A heritage
That Heaven hath blessed
By many an olden token !
The one day when the peasant feels
His weary hand at rest and free ;
When he may whisper where he kneels,
This day is left to heaven and me !

XXXVIII.

Prelude of rest
To come,—when fall
The folds of pall for ever,
On grief and pain,
And care and quest,
And every vain endeavour !
And work, the fount of rest, is still ;
And busy head and cunning hand,
The arm of strength, the stubborn will,
Have left their labours to the Land.

XXXIX.

The rest that brings
Not rust ; the time
When wild doves' wings are folden ;
The hour before
The skylark soar,
With midnight's chime scarce tolden !
The weary horses know the close
Of their long week of weariness ;
The children say the very crows
On Sunday look you in the face.

XL.

And surely each
Good influence
Doth teach a larger duty,
A clearer sense
Of mercy, part
Of even Art and Beauty.
This ancient periodic peace
Imparts instinctive sense of ways,
Till nature seeks this day's release,
Her mute unconscious mode of praise.

XLI.

And over all,
The homely bell
Rings out to tell the story
Of ancient ways,
Of ancient days,
Of rest from thraldom hoary :
And 'mid that lull from toil and wrong,
Come from of old the far-off strains
Of that immortal stream of song
That rose on old Chaldean plains.

XLII.

It rings through all
The kindly link
That neighbour ties to neighbour ;
It flings o'er all
The sunny blink
Of rest, the prize of labour :
For neighbourhood with homely folk
Goes hand in hand with kin,
And helps the back to bear the yoke,
The hand to work and win.

XLIII.

Through all their homes
The sound of bells
So softly swells this morning ;
With memories
Of home-sweet ties
It comes at every turning,—
Of bridal wreath and infant bloom,
And maybe buds of hope laid low ;
It blessed in gladness and in gloom
Their fathers long ago.

XLIV.

And friendship left
In boy-love's place,
The world's dull way to lighten—
The purple weft
Of pleasantness,
Life's web of grey to brighten—
Remains, and dies not with the dead :
The elder men young faces scan,
And say, while patting some young head,
Your father was an honest man.

XLV.

I see them yet,—
Where distance blends
The things I do not care to sever,—
The men who were
My father's friends,
And I'll forget them never :
When like the hush of some still wood,
A breath of wind on some still sea,
Rise up the silent multitude
Amid the hushed serenity.

XLVI.

One spot of earth
For each man's birth,
One spot for each one's resting-place;
But mind for mind
Takes wider reach,
With ties of binding kindliness;
Not judging rites, or prayer or praise,
Or lands where Christian people dwell,
But loving still our Scottish ways,
Old Scotland and her Sabbath bell.

XLVII.

Faith knows no change,
Though forms grow strange.
High in its golden regions
Yon skylark's song
Hath oft and long
Rung down the old religions:
But Faith that through the ages flows,
From one pure fount that runs not dry,
Is evermore: no change it knows
On Horeb or on Calvary.

XLVIII.

Sing on, sweet bird,
Ring on, old bell,
In tones of ordered meetness ;
Though sweet birds sing
And sweet bells ring,
Your well-accorded sweetness
I would not give for all the choirs
That wake the heavens from sea to sea ;
They link us with those hero sires
Who taught us what brave men should be.

XLIX.

And what they were,
And what they won
Through many a year of sorrow,
The old kirk bell
To-day will tell,
Will tell anon to-morrow.
It rings throughout the long, long past,
In sounds that come from far away,
As if it caught when it was cast,
The tones of some diviner day.

L.

Diviner ! nay,
Though times long gone
We may deem aye the holier,
We see the high
And grand alone,
And ne'er descry the lowlier.
The victor's palm, the martyr's crown,
Conceal the mass of common things ;.
While Justice winneth no renown,
And Truth has silent wings.

LI.

Ring out, sweet bell—
Ring out, and tell
We're neither changed, nor changing,—
From good old ways,
Of good old days,
Estranged, nor yet estranging ;
For nobler grows the land for you,
Where your bold voice is heard ;
The heart and hand more trusty true,
The braver thought and word.

LII.

And far and near
Your sounding lip,
In circles wide and wider,
Will ring where'er
A British ship
Hath British hands to guide her.
And o'er the land and o'er the sea
May blessings keep you sound and well,
Amid a faithful land to be
Their Old Kirk Bell !

CHILDREN IN THE WOODS.

" Pueri ludentes, Rex eris, aiunt,
Si recte facies."—HORACE.

The boys in their sports say, If you do well you shall be a king.

Go gather sunbeams where they lie
　On every hillside sleeping;
And put them where they will not die,
　Within your young heart's keeping.
They paint with light, with loving hand, the blossom
　while it's blowing,
　They tune the lays of every land, and bless where'er
　　they fall;
Keep every day, like Summer gay, for yellow Autumns
　　glowing,
　For happy hearts have summer aye, and sunshine
　　over all.

Then merry all—go merrily,
   And happy foot go free,
With laughter ringing cheerily;
   I would not stint your glee :
Wake up, you gladsome voices, till the grand old
   wood rejoices !
Let beauty claim her kindred where the lordly
   Summer's hand
His path of light is spreading for the bride that he is
   wedding;
Go all, and greet the rosy Queen, the Queen of
   Summer-land.

The primrose blooms for Easter-tide,
   The daffodil for May;
But June is lordly Summer's bride,
   And this her bridal day.
And who but you, as pure as dew, as true as ye are
   tender,
So light of heart, should bear your part, amid her
   bridal cheer?
And who but you, to life so new, should dance amid
   her splendour,—
Should rise with living rapture through the radiance
   of the year?

Then dance away the merry day,
Your meed of music bringing,
Where household cares hush half the lay
The birds were lately singing;
The Robin in his summer haunt, his woodland place
of wooing,
Has all forgot the welcome note that sang away the
snow;
The Cushat coos among the firs, the green Cuckoo
cuckooing,
Your little mimic voices stirs to music as ye go.

See there, the glimpse of grassy dales
Is gleaming through the larches,
And here, like dim cathedral aisles,
The gloom of beechen arches;
The heather-blush is barely seen, the bud is on
the thorn;
The woodbines o'er the snow-white gean their first
fresh garlands fling;
And there the flush of noontide rays, and here the
dawn of morn,
Where fainting fair anemones have vanished with
the Spring.

And many a flower is blowing
 To the fulness of its noon,
Where the Summer king is going
 With his queenly lady June.
Her cheek is like the apple-bloom before it opens
 fairly ;
 She strews the ground with flowers around, with
 ever-radiant hand ;
Her smiles that all lie where they fall, she scatters late
 and early ;
 For those who greet the rosy Queen when coming
 through the land.

Then wake the gladsome greenwood way,
 With all your young delight ;
I've seen your fathers' hearts as gay,
 Your mothers' eyes as bright.
And they are all the gayer, all the brighter are their
 eyes,
 For days they spent in merriment, among the woods
 of old ;
And they are all the gayer all, for happy thoughts
 that rise,
 And far-off hours like these recall all clad in robes
 of gold.

 C

Some brown as nuts in nutting days,
    Some blushing red as maples ;
They rolled about the heather braes
    Like rosy-cheekèd apples ;
And up and down the woodland brown the merry
    band went dancing,
    Their hearts as light as any bird's to memory and
        me ;
As sunset-beams on sparkling streams their bright
    young eyes were glancing ;
    Their voices sweet and happy feet kept time with
        tuneful glee.

And hope may pour its richest store
    With every promise true ;
Yet golden halcyons shine no more
    Like those that shine on you.
And ye will seek, as I have sought, for beauty's fad-
    ing traces,
    The footprints of the Summers where ye danced in
        other years ;
And find that sunshine never dies when shed on
    happy faces,
    But lives through lifelong memories, though may-
        be fringed with tears.

Then dance away with merry din,
    I love your laughter dearly;
The linnet on his moorland whin
    Could never sing so clearly.
The golden thrush, within his bush, the blackbird on
    his tree,
    Have kept their sweet love-songs to greet the bridal
      joys of June;
And far away the skylark's lay rings o'er the lowan
    lea;
    Oh, happy song of happy hearts with song and
      heart in tune!

The rathe buds, with their ruby lips,
    To Summer's kisses cling;
The larches' tender finger-tips
    Wave farewell to the Spring;
The chestnut's hyacinthine flower, the ever-fragrant
    haw,
    Are shedding balms through sun and shower, and
      beauty where they stand;
The ancient oaks, like brave old kings, who kept the
    world in awe,
    All greet with love the rosy Queen, the Queen of
      Summer-land.

Then make the merry greenwood ring
  With voices sweet to hear,
As songs that fairy maidens sing
  At milking of the deer.
It is the time when Summer, all his golden glory
  shedding,
  His joys on every comer, all his love on sea and
  shore,   .
His path of light is spreading, for the bride that he is
  wedding,
  His radiant Queen in bridal sheen, his loved one
  evermore.

Then dance through all their rosy reign,
  Be merry while you may;
You'll never dance so young again,
  Though dancing every day.
The old divine emotion that is throbbing. every-
  where,
Is waking into beauty, and is breaking into song:
The ever-young whose raptures sprung when Eden
  first was fair,
  Makes hearts as light, and eyes as bright, and
  blithe 's the day is long.

There's joy in every blossom-fold,
　　There's peace among the leaves ;
And all the sunshine turns to gold
　　Among the harvest sheaves.
But all the harvests are not when the grain is waving
　　yellow,
And brown October apples in their ruddy ripeness
　　fall !
Then gather sunshine while you may, to make your
　　Autumn mellow,
And let you keep, in after-day, an open heart for
　　all.

THE RIVER.

" Ille
Labitur et labetur in omne volubilis ævum."—HORACE.

FROM the bosom of the mountain,
From the silent lands of night,
Sparkles up the infant fountain,
Crystal clear and crowned with light;
With a gentle tinkle ringing,
        Sweetly singing,
        Ever bringing,
Freshful radiance to the sight;
Like a happy-hearted maiden,
Robes of golden joy arrayed in,
Dancing to the inner music
Of her own young heart's delight.
Upwards to the summer skies,
Laughing love, with starry eyes;
Downwards to the mossy slope,
Darting free and full of hope;

And the list'ning air it fills
With the tinkling of its rills;
Ancient rocks look blithe to hear it,
Heather-bells bloom fresher near it,
And a thousand charms endear it
To the old paternal hills.

And downward it patters,
And outward it scatters
Its silvery waters to gladden the land;
And childlike it chatters,
And gleefully clatters,
And murmurs of matters
We don't understand.
But there's meaning in music, whatever it be,
From the sough of the wind to the sound of the sea;
In the hum of the vale, and the hush of the woods,
In the voice of the stream, and the change of its moods,
In the thunder that rolls o'er the midsummer day,
In the murmur that wakes when the storm is away,
In the lowing of kine, and the carol of birds,
In a wilderness teeming with eloquent words;
And nature is moving in worshipful glee
To the sound of its music whatever it be.
And gleaming and glancing,
The streamlet goes dancing,

And singing afar from the spot where it rose,
And flowing and falling, it grows as it goes;
Gladsomely culling, it gathers its brothers
From many a fountain;
And down through the mists from the clefts of the
mountain,
The slowly-wrung tribute of tarrying snows.

And onward it dashes,
And outward it plashes,
And rushes and flashes
So fleet in its flight,
And so bright in its light;
Brawling and brattling,
Romping and rattling,
Rollicking, frolicking, dancing downwards,
With a persistence
Defying resistance,
In all the unconscious compulsion of might.
Away and away, through the woodlands careering,
As clear as the day; like a sunbeam appearing
In darkness; a voice in the solitude, singing
A song of rejoicing, and evermore bringing,
With many a murmur and musical fall,
A hope to the hopeless,
A joy to the joyless,

A love to the loveless,
A beauty to all.

Now the birch is beginning to grow on its brink,
Where the deer of the mountain come downward to
    drink,
And the shepherd's dog barks from some lone sum-
    mer shealing,
Some neighbourless home, of the moorland revealing.
Now faster and faster flows on the fleet river,
Increasing, unceasing, rejoicing for ever ;
Through forests that wave with the honours of ages,
Ravines with the pines on their tottering ledges ;
Through hollows unblest by the sunshine of heaven,
Through rocks that the wrath of the torrent has riven.
And onward and downward it rushes and rages,
With headlong rapidity into the linn,
Rumbling and tumbling, in foamy confusion ;
        Boiling and pouring,
        And toiling and roaring,
Filling the mind with a horrid illusion
Of spirits in trouble with sorrow and sin—
And all with a deep, subterranean din.

Then, resting awhile from the toils of the fight,
It bounds through the land in the strength of its might,

Like a steed of the desert, all fearless and free,
All foaming and white with its warrior glee.
It passes the glens with a clarion call,
And gathers its crystalline tribute from all,
Where worshipful mountains so solemnly stand,
And old immemorial oaks of the land
Cry, " We are but children to these and to thee,
Thou bountiful daughter of mountain and sea."
And down by the woodlands so dreary and deep,
And down by the valleys all dotted with sheep,
And over the shallows, and over the sand,
It sings like a joy in the heart of the land.

O maiden ! O maiden !
Thy beauty arrayed in,
It comes through the long summer sunshine like thee,
With happiness singing,
Its merriment ringing,
Its radiance flinging
Profusely and free.
It kisses, caresses, and blesses the dearest—
Gladdens, O maiden, the next to the nearest ;
Covers with graces
The gloomiest places :
The light of the woodland, the loved of the lea,
O maiden, it comes in its beauty like thee !

Beauteous river, gentle river,
River of the golden sands,
Like a silver band enfolding,
Grassy leas and golden lands,
Which the ancient hills are holding
In the hollows of their hands.
Down beside the fields of story,
Sung in many an ancient lay—
Down by keep and castle hoary,
Down by gorges grim and grey—
With a noble undulation,
Ringing down from far away,
Like a song of early glory,
Sung through many an ancient day.
Through the woodlands calm and shady,
Softly, sweetly, gently, slowly,
Moving like a graceful lady,
With a look serene and holy,
With a beauteous melancholy,
In the crystal of her eyes.
Moving onwards, sweet and simple,
Through the sunny nook, its dimple
Gleams from out its foamy wimple,
Cloudless as the cloudless skies.
Each glance a glimpse of heaven discloses,
Holy things and thoughts revealing,

Safe where sunshine interposes,
Like a flush of human feeling;
Or where trees and woodland roses
Wreathe it round with garlands fair,
Softly, sweetly, gently flowing,
Round a chastened radiance throwing,
Like a saintly lady going
To the holy house of prayer.
Down beside the churchyard sighing,
With an accent sad and low,
To a dirge its cadence dying,
O'er the many, lowly lying,
Those who loved it long ago.
But the little temple telleth
Of the sacred hope that dwelleth,
Of the bliss that never faileth,
Hid behind the pall of woe;
And a song of joy it raises—
Anthems full of ceaseless praises,
Sung through all its wayward mazes,
Tuned to accents sweet and slow.
On it flows in stately beauty,
On it goes in humble peace,
Nobly, for it does its duty,
Humbly, in the land's increase.

Wearily washing through meadowy reaches,
Weltering under the roots of the beeches,
Sighing in gusts where the quivering sedges
Shiver as freshets curl over its edges.

    Onward it urges
    Its flood through the gorges,
And dashes its foam to their pine-covered verges;
    And seething in surges,
    It brightly emerges
To light on the broad and the bountiful plain.

    On river, bright river,
    A blessing for ever:
    Oh, blest is the Giver,
    The gift is so free.
    It flows through the valleys
    So beautiful always,
    The land's crystal chalice
    From mountain to sea.

Now far o'er the meadow the cattle are lowing,
  And far away herd-boys are whistling together;
While hay-makers homeward are merrily going.
  There's joy in the breath of the sweet summer
    weather,

The odours of blossoms and music of birds;
And the air whispers peace in a voice without words.
The river in solemn serenity glideth,
    Sleeplike, but sleepless—and silent as nature
When moulding her manifold wonders, she hideth
    The might of her hand and the height of her stature
In graceful quiescence and flowery array;
    Concealing the mystical spirit of grandeur,
And guiding the rapt one, the art-fingered angel
    Of Beauty, and moving in passionless splendour,
She comes o'er the land, like a blessèd evangel,
    Reflecting the Holy One's presence alway.
The mountains are silent, in deep adoration,
    The valleys in rapture with music and light,
And o'er us the glorious guide of creation
    Is treading his crystalline pathway, as bright
As first when he shed on the rivers of Eden
    The glory that gladdened their Sabbath of rest;
And softly and stilly the river is flowing
    Between the green copses that shadow its border;
And hereaway glooming and thereaway glowing
    Amid the green woodlands' delicious disorder,
As moves the broad sun through the golden-boughed
        gardens,
    And down to the amber-arched halls of the west.

And as the blue mountains are fading from sight,
   The song of the waters is rising alone
With mightier voice through the silence of night,
   When all the sweet singers of sunshine are gone.
      Rushing away with its musical song,
      Singing a lullaby all the night long,
      Murmuring low by the woodland deep,
      Babbling aloud o'er the pebbly steep,
        And the night is all its own.   ·
It tells not the lord in his castle grand,—
   The wealth of the bountiful meadow is mine;
Nor says to the farmer that tills the green land,
   I'm filling the corn, and feeding the kine.
The old merry mill in the midst of the trees,
It drives without multure, it craves not for fees;
Nor says to the thousands that dwell on its brink,
Lo! I am the fountain whose waters ye drink,—
The light of the valley, the wealth of the lea,
That shines ever fairly, whose gifts are so free ;
That brings from the mountains the treasures of snow,
When little lone streams of the summer are low—
And fresh from the forests' endearing embrace,
And from the bare moorlands all gleaming with dew,
The silvery wealth of the wilderness,
      A tribute of love for you.

THE EVERGREEN.

A SONG OF THE DOUBLE WINTER.

THE Oak and the Pine and the Holly-tree
   Are the joy of the winter land ;
For the glossy green is so fair to see,
   And the brave old Oak so grand.
The old Oak-tree has his kingly crown,
   And the Holly her winter glow ;
And we'll gather the green leaves and the brown
    For the garland of the snow,
                   Brave heart—
For the garland of the snow.

That they die in their youth whom the gods belove,
   Was an ancient belief, we are told ;
And 'tis true, for those locks of silver prove
   There are hearts that can ne'er grow old.
The cloud may come with the rain behind,
   But the greener the green leaves grow ;

And the Oak-tree laughs at the winter's wind,
   And the Holly at the snow,
                 Brave heart—
And the Holly at the snow.

With the brown oak-leaves we will wreathe your head,
   With the holly-boughs your room,
With a gleam of the life that the ancients led,
   With their feasts made bright with bloom.
As little they tell you—the wreath or the song—
   As they tell where the summers go,
With their sunshine short and their memories long
   That to-night in these bright eyes glow,
                 Brave heart—
That to-night in these bright eyes glow.

They are glowing with love in their mellow light,
   They are full of their ancient joy;
It is fourscore years and ten this night
   Since they shone in the merry boy;
But the gladsome songs of the summer's prime
   We hear, though the green leaves flow,
And the oak-leaves tell us in winter time
   Where the good men's summers go,
                 Brave heart —
Where the good men's summers go.

D

The stateliest tree we have seen cut down,
  And the blight of the loveliest flower,
That the smiles of May or the kisses of June
  Will gladden to life no more :
And the true and the tender have vanished away,
  As their blossoms began to blow ;
May they live in our hearts, in their beauty for aye,
  When our heads are like the snow,
                    Brave heart—
When our heads are like the snow.

The clouds might come and the tears might fall
  As the busy years passed by,
But the sun shone brightly over all
  In the blue of a cloudless sky.
Shone over all with its golden light
  On the path where the bright ones go ;
And it shines, I think, on thy head to-night,
  With its crown of stainless snow,
                    Brave heart—
With its crown of stainless snow.

Thus we sing of the Oak and the Evergreen
  When the land is winter bare,
For they tell us of summer's golden sheen,
  And the flowers in her yellow hair ;

Of the leaves that the winter cannot part
    From the joy of their native bough,
And when youth never fades in the Grandsire's heart;
    Oh ! blest is the head of snow,
                Brave heart—
Oh ! blest is the head of snow !

THE SONGS OF OTHER YEARS.

DEAR lady, touch that chord again,
  And sing again that simple lay;
To me an old familiar strain
  Of long ago and far away.
I heard it in the Highland north—
  The land where song lies bathed in tears--
And still it calls old feelings forth,
  Like many a song of other years.

Like many a mother's saintly hymn,
  Whose lingering tones can ne'er depart,
Though ears be deaf, and eyes be dim,
  And worldly ways have seared the heart;
Like many a smile of early love
  That still and aye the loved one wears,
They come the heart's deep fount to move,
  The pleasant songs of other years.

They wake sweet lips in silent lands,
  Bring back the light of loving eyes,
Bring back the touch of faithful hands,
  Bring back the blue of former skies,
And merry evening times of old,
  All fairer through the mist of tears,
With gems to light their gracious gold,—
  The sad sweet songs of other years.

The mirth of old may make us sad,
  But may it never make us grieve;
The day most gloriously glad
  Grows tender in its dewy eve;
But evening, sweet as any day,
  With all its heaven of radiant spheres,
And joys that long have passed away,
  Come back in song from other years.

II.

NOTES AND ECHOES

"The Heaven of the poets, or the primitive ground of the whole heathen mythology, is in its origin nothing more than an instructive and innocent way of writing; but stupidly mistaken and grossly understood, in the sense it offered to the eye, instead of being taken in that it was intended to offer to the mind."—*The History of the Heavens*, by the ABBE PLUCHE.

ISIS.

" They say that the Egyptians celebrate the festival of Isis in that part of
the year in which she bewails Osiris; that the Nile then begins to ascend;
and that the vulgar of the natives say that the tears of Isis cause the Nile
to increase and irrigate the fields."—PAUSANIAS' *Description of Greece.*

DARK Isis of the Silver Horn
Is moving in her sorrow through the night,
Alone and widowed, in a world forlorn,
  By life and light.
A shadowy form of mystery and might,
With cloudy garments trailing far behind,
By deep dark waters and by silent shore,
  With all her handmaids gone,
  And of the kind
Sweet sympathies of kindred having none,
Nor any living thing to bless her sight,
Nor any joy, nor any hope; but o'er
The whole wide waste of death she moves alone !

And thus she walked, with ever-silent tread,
Amid the wreck of all that was so fair;
The night-cloud mingling with her cloudy hair,
Half trailing o'er her dim soft silver horn:
When all the light of heaven was overcast,
And all the blossom of her life was shed,
And her great heart the grave of all the past,
And she the only mourner left to mourn.

But lo! from out the darkness came a cry,—
Osiris! unto thee a child is born—
A man-child to my lord, this night of woe.
Where is thy glory now? where dost thou lie?
Beneath the waters of the mournful sea?
Or where the death-winds blow
Upon the voiceless wastes of Arimi?

And down amid the darkness she has gone,
With silent steps, majestical and slow,
And the wan glimmer of her silver horn,
And her pale child of sorrow newly born;
Amid the trouble of the waters wild:
And sat her down beside the vacant throne
                    Alone
With desolation and her child.

And there arose a long dread cry of Woe !
  Woe unto Typhon the abhorred,
The unblessed spirit of the hungry deep,
That rose from the abyss and slew my lord
  In the confiding glory of his sleep !
    Whither shall Isis go,
Amid the pathless wastes of night and crime ?
The beautiful Osiris is no more !
The day is dead ! the night doth know no sleep !
And Typhon's scaly folds all curl and creep
About the darkness of the tomb of time
  By sea and slimy shore.

For woe and darkness are for evermore :
From out of which arose the abhorrent worm,
And of the beauty that Osiris wore,
He stole a part to clothe his formless form.
    And thus anon,
  He crept in that disguise
By shadowy trees, and mountains vast and hoar,
In borrowed glory fit for gods alone :
For lo ! the light of young Osiris' eyes
Made all things lovely that it shone upon.

And I who weep
Was watching in the west
My lord, amid the grandeur of his throne,
Sinking asleep
In the pavilions of his kingly rest ;
When rose a moving glimmer far away
Of circling rings, uncoiling faintly fair,
The death-light of decay.
In cloudless calm from that cerulean height,
Where I my loving vigil used to keep,
I gazed in wonder, silent and alone,
When Typhon's hateful front flashed from the night,
With small red eyes, and cold wet snaky hair,   -
And smote my lord, and pierced his snowy breast;
And desolation fell on land and deep,
And all my joy was gone.

And all the long night through
Her solitary moaning by the sea
Rose with the wail thereof, which sadder grew,
Lashed into agony
By old-night winds that day-dawn never knew,
That never fanned the forest's fragrant tree,
Nor drank the living breath of pleasant lands,
Nor heard the homeward lowing of the kine,
. Nor saw the sunshine swell the purpling vine,

Nor reaper's song had heard, nor household glee,
Nor low-voiced Pity with her tears of dew;
But moaned of hungry seas and homeless sands,
From out the ghostly wastes of Arimi.

And lo ! the young child grew,
Even in the darkness of life desolate,
With all the innate vigour of a god;
And he the bow of great Osiris drew,
Which Isis found upon the midnight shore,
And bare his quiver and his darts of fate,
Tipped with eternal fire from the abode
Where, at the root of all the ages gone,
With eyeless faces, motionless as stone,
Necessity and Night sit evermore.
They searched that sad night long,
Whereof the dark duration lies untold,
The sole survivors of the world's wide wrong
In those dread days of old.
And as they wandered over wilds unknown,
Where never foot the rugged path had trod,
Where silence seemed itself to sit and moan,
Where never more could joy have its abode,
They saw a terror on the holy throne,—
A darkness darker than the night unrolled,—
Its slimy coils evolving, fold on fold.

And lo ! the young child bent
Up to his ear Osiris' golden bow,
          And quivering sent
The arrow tipt with the eternal fire,
Hissing and wet, into the monster's brow.
A cry arose of wrath, and fear, and pain,
And with it came a pale light o'er the sea—
A faint sweet glimmer from Osiris' crown ;
And as if Night the rising Dawn had rent
          In trembling twain,
Fell Typhon howling, down, and down, and down,
Upon the ghostly wastes of Arimi ;
Shaking the ground and surging up the main !

          In her dim dawn of joy
Stood Isis trembling, while with one white arm
          She clasped her boy,
And with her gleaming hand threw back her hair
From off her brow, imperishably fair ;
And in an agony of new alarm,
For hope itself seemed hopelessly divine,
Still struggling from the death-grasp of despair,
She gazed in awe, with blanchèd lips apart,
And eyes of light, and tears, that seemed to shine
With all that ever touched a woman's heart,
          Across the throbbing brine ;

And from its breast
She saw Osiris rise,
With broken diadem and golden hair.
She saw the loving glory of his eyes,
That gazed upon her from a wave's white crest.
So pale and yet so fair !
Pale from his wounds, but yet divinely fair,
With the immortal beauty of his race !
My lord, she cried, and through the waters wild
In joy she rushed and to her bosom pressed,
The wounded god, and kissed his pale, pale face,
In rapture o'er and o'er,
And to his loving eyes she gave the child,
Who kept his watch upon the lonely shore.

And Beauty bloomed again ;
And Love and Peace
Blessed all the lands where Woe had held its reign;
And Nature, gladdened by the sweet release,
Renewed the raptures of her early morn,
Burst into singing, till the joyous strain
From clime to clime o'er all the world was borne.
The hills beheld with all their old delight,
The loving trees their rugged limbs adorn ;
And rivers flowed in beauty to the main ;

And from the desert came the songs of praise,
    And from the plain ;
And from the ocean, now no longer white,
Came hymnal murmurs solemn aye and sweet.

For beauty grew, in all its wondrous ways,
    Beneath Osiris' gaze ;
And queenly Isis, with her silver horn,
Moved in her gracious splendour through the night,
With all her handmaids gleaming in her train,
With jewelled brows and ever-silent feet ;
And oft when Nature felt the throb of pain
From Typhon's wounds, and murmured of the days
When she her robe of virgin beauty wore,
She knew the god who broke the tyrant's chain
Would make his early victory complete
    For evermore.

NOTE.—" It was sufficiently obvious that the principal Egyptian feasts had a relation to the dismal alteration which the Flood had introduced into nature. Then they lamented with Isis the loss of the visible ruler of the universe, who had been taken from them and killed by a dragon which rose from under the earth, a water-monster. They rejoiced over the resurrection of Osiris, but he was no longer the same, and had lost his strength."—ABBE PLUCHE.

   .   .   .   .

"What contributed most to the seduction of the Egyptians was the frequent appearance of a crescent moon, on Isis' head-dress. Thence they took occasion to give it out that Osiris' wife and the common mother of the Egyptians had the moon for her dwelling-place."—*Ibid.*

" Horus, the son of Osiris, the symbolical child, . . . representing work and industry, . . . called the son of the star of the day, because husbandry can do nothing without the sun."—*Ibid.*

HEPHÆSTUS.

I.—IN THE SEA.

" She and Eurynome my griefs redressed,
And soft received me on their wat'ry breast."
—*Iliad :* Pope's Translation.

HEPHÆSTUS, from Olympus cast,
  Lay wounded on the strand,
When a milk-white sea-maid wandered past,
  Like a sunbeam o'er the sand :
With her songs so sweet, and her white, white feet,
  Half lost in the loving sea ;
And wood and hill lay hushed and still,
  In the far-off songs of Eurynomè.

And long and well she tended him,
  And sang in her heart's delight :
And all within her sea-cave dim
  To him was Olympian bright.
He gazed in her face in his lowliness,
  He sighed at her maiden glee,
As he sang her strain, with its wild refrain—
  Oh, the flower of all for Eurynomè.

E

He built her a hall, with its crystal dome,
　　Over golden spandrils flung ;
And the waters round her ocean home
　　In crystal silence hung.
And he led her o'er the sapphire floor,
　　In the wondrous light of the sea ;
And his sad looks said to the sweet sea-maid,
　　Will you love me now, Eurynomè ?

She sang with joy, and clapped her hands,
　　As she danced all round about ;
But it was not to her like the moonlit sands,
　　When the evening tide is out.
She sparkled and sang and the sea-hall rang,
　　And her yellow locks floated free ;
Oh, joy for joy, and love for love,
　　But the flower of all for Eurynomè.

He wandered away in his lowliness,
　　And he made her a crown of gems,
More bright than ever he gleaned to grace
　　The Olympian diadems.
He had gathered them far, where the rarest are,
　　In the wondrous light of the sea ;
And his sad looks said to the sweet sea-maid,
　　Will ye love me now, Eurynomè ?

But she sang as she shone on her ruby throne,
    Like a star in its own sweet light ;—
It's the dew to the rose that the sun shines on,
    It's the stars to the moon at night :
But it's not so fair as my yellow hair,
    Nor so bright as myself, said she ;
And joy for joy, and love for love,
    But the flower of all for Eurynomè.

He had the skill and he had the will,
    And he had the heart for all ;
There was not a wish but he would fulfil
    For the joy of the sea-maid's hall.
He made her a lyre, whose golden wire
    Never woke to grief or glee ;
And his sad looks said to the sweet sea-maid,
    Will ye love me now, Eurynomè ?

But he woke no chord, he called no tone
    Of rapture from its strings :
Oh, she said, but I know of the nobler One
    Who can do all the nobler things ;
And she sang the lays of another's praise,
    Of a mightier god than he ;
Oh, joy for joy, and it's love for love,
    But the flower of all for Eurynomè.

Hephæstus spake, and blushed like wine;—
  He will love you while love is new,
And leave you to pine for a love like mine,
  And humble heart and true !
His love is a day of love, and away ;
  And the calm sweet homes of the sea,
And the soft sea light, he will turn to night,
  And the golden joys of Eurynomè.

II.—IN LEMNOS.

" His sinewy arms incessant place
  The eternal anvil on its massy base."
       —*Odyssey:* Pope's Translation.

The forges all blow red and white,
  The clanging anvils ring ;
As up through the darkness, down through the light,
  The thousand hammers swing.
The murky faces rise and fall,
  Ever red by the furnace, dark by the wall,
'Mid roar and ring, and fierce fire-spray,
  The anvils clanging night and day,
    And the Fire-god ruling all.

'Mid smoke and flame,
   And ring and roar,
He moves about low-voiced and lame,
   In the light of the luminous ore.
For grief has touched his master-hand
   With a strange sweet power at its command—
A wondrous power, a nameless grace,
   And a more than woman's tenderness;
And the scorn of lesser gods than he
   Is forgiven in his humility.
He envies not the pleasure,
   Nor the glory of the gods,
Nor the Elysian leisure
   Of their ever-blest abodes;
Nor the crimson light of their radiant halls—
Though where but for him were the ruby walls?
Nor the crowns that on their foreheads shine—
Though where but for him were the crowns divine?
Nor the juice from heavenly grapes expressed
In the cups of the icy amethyst
     That he made to hold their wine.

The forges all blow red and white,
   And ring the anvils all,
As up through darkness, down through the light,
   The hammers rise and fall.

The purpose of strength gives perfection apace,
The passion of fire, the fashion of grace ;
With the red bronze clanging change on change
In the birthplace of beauty, where beauty is strange.
The trident of Neptune, the sceptre of Jove,
That awe to the dust the kingliest race,
Are the fruits of his labours of duty and love ;
For deep in his lurid cavern dim
Is his brave work dearer far to him
   Than the sunniest hours of idleness.

   And his was the bolt,
    When Olympus seemed lost,
   That crushed the revolt
    Of the demigod host.
He saw them aloft on Mount Pelion pass,
While their mighty limbs gleamed in the sunset like
  brass ;
He saw them smote down, reeling back on the skies,
With a solemn despair in their sorrowful eyes.
His was the red thunder-fire—his it is still—
That blackened the valley and shattered the hill,
And clove through the death-wrack a pathway of
  peace ;
As the rage of the Pontic was hushed by release,
And the waters of Helle come calm to our feet ;—

As the storm - wave that breaks on the bulwark of
    Crete,
      Is a joy to the sunny Cyclades.

    And his brave hand brings,
      From their place of birth
    At the roots of the mountain, the terrible things
      That rage in the inner earth.
They bow before his grimy face,
They come to his hand in gentleness,
Where the fiery mid-earth torrents pour
A flaming sea on a burning shore ;
For he rules where their sulphurous fumes disgorge,
As he does by the light of his own red forge.
The demiurgic bellows blows,
    In the flame of his roaring furnaces ;
And into the moulds the metal flows,
    For a thousand things of strength and grace.
And the sleepless work of the sleepless arm
        Goes on alway,
        By night and by day,
'Mid the ring and the roar and the fierce fire-spray !
While bare to the waist the Cyclops swarm
All here and there, with a purpose clear ;
And a dusky iridescence glows
On the molten metal's creaming face,

Like the dolphin's side in its dying throes.
And out of the mass at the Fire-god's will
Come the things of hope and the things of fear,
The things of force and the things of skill ;
And he forges and burnishes day and night,
And all in his blind demiurgic might.

And he fashioned the golden arms
That the great Apollo wore,—
Till his bow-string rang with lyric charms,
And he wore the sword no more.
For mightier far is the singer's song
Than the sword and spear to shield from wrong ;
For he links the whole earth clime to clime,
All in the light of a holier time,
Over the mountains, over the sea,
Linking the wide earth silently.
But strike with a will while the metal glows,—
As the hammers ring so the good work grows ;
And the loving to labour, the patient to bear,
Is lifting his brave head everywhere,
But not in sloth or in weariness,
But all with the lands that his labours bless ;
And he hears the song that the singer sings,
And he sings it o'er while his hammer rings
Over the mountains and over the sea,
Linking the whole earth silently.

III.—TRIUMPHANT.

" Vulcan perpetually imitating the intellectual energy of Minerva in the fabrication of the sensible universe, . . . which Apollo harmonises."—Notes on PAUSANIAS.

The days of thought, though lost in pain,
Are they not ransomed back again
By thought and labour ? Even so :
Though sorrows oftener come than go,
The living day thy soul hath lit
  By light supernal
  Is eternal,
No night can overshadow it.

So struggling through the vanished years,
Doth Hope, the soul of all their springs,
Dart upwards, shaking off the tears
Of ages from her rosy wings.
Each race bequeaths its better part,
The noblest aim in all its heart,
To each successor, like the torch
Borne in the course by Athens' youth,
Through rites, and games, and gleams of truth,
From Pallas' shrine to Vulcan's porch.

What age hath kept the sacred fire !
What age hath left it to expire !

The one is shining in its light,
The other lost amid the night.
While ages pass and nations fall,
One living truth doth ransom all
From cold oblivion ; though men grope
But by the morning star of hope
Before the sun, for truths that lie
In some dim Pagan prophecy.
The grand Minerval light intense,
The clear Terrene intelligence,
  The one creative,
  One formative,
Both joining things of thought and sense,
Draw closer in our age and clime
The mythic links of elder time ;
Till, wrought in brass by cunning hands,
The truth from nature's heart expressed,
In broad interpretation stands,
Majestically manifest.

The golden chain of links divine,
 Let down of old through all the sky,
Was but a faint and far-off sign
 Of more than laws of unity.
The light of thought half hid in dreams,
 Of ancient thaumaturgic lore,

Is broadening out in purer beams,
  Whose living truth is living power.

The King whose ruby palace walls
Were rarest of Olympian halls,
His starry dome have we not seen ?
Have we not blest ? Hath it not been
A wonder in a wondrous age,
A splendour in a splendid page
      Of our land's story
      Set in glory,
And glowing through the summer fair,
  Like sunrise on an Eastern sea,
Where widening splendour everywhere
  Is centred in intensity ?
What land but sent its treasures rare,
  What far-off sea but sent its spoils,
What industry but gathered there
  The marvel of its toils ?
Whate'er the wealth, whate'er the land,
  The good work had the same old source ;
The might of lame Hephæstus' hand,
  The old Vulcanian force,
But swayed by that harmonic god,
  In whom each mundane reason lies

In beautifying man's abode
  With all things good, and fair, and wise.
He brought his works from east and west,
Of every age and clime the best;
The children of his subject fire,
The silent thunders of his sire,
And forms of strength and symmetry
Which tell us each in its degree
In perfect means to purpose live,
The graces nothing else can give:
The powers more rich than mines of gold,
That make man's strength a thousandfold—
His perils less, his path more sure,
And give new pleasures to the poor.
Historic beauty wore a crown
Of more than its antique renown:
The wonders of Arachne's loom,
The more than Tyrian purple bloom,
And fairer gems from every shore
Than those that young Harmonia wore.
We deemed it then a fane of peace,
To which men came in joyfulness
From every region to behold
That dream of crystal, light, and gold.
Though swords have oft been red since then,
And redder still may be again,

With some great nation's voiceless woe,—
The growth of mighty things is slow,—
A fount of Peace it still will be,
Linking the whole earth silently.

Though oft the burning edge of strife
   Repels with pain the touch of love,
Through many a tender tie of life,
   Of hearts and homes, his hand doth move.
He gives with swords and ringing shields
The sickle for the harvest fields ;
And though he forge the arms that grace
His rival, Mars the merciless,
His are a hundred peaceful ways
That cheer the sturdy craftsman's days.
His are the iron ocean towers,
The guardians of a hundred shores,
With Neptune's trident at the prow,
And slumbering thunders hushed below.
Their path is tracked by pearly foam,
Across the ancient ocean deeps ;
      Amid their splendours
      The defenders
Of all the sacred fire that keeps
Our glory bright at home.

The wondrous powers which have their birth
Deep in the iron womb of earth,
The spirit of volcanic fire,
And all engulfing earthquake dire,
The old laborious Fire-king brings,
All tamed into familiar things.
O'er every sea they cleave their way
From shore to shore; and day by day
They spread the light of better climes,
The brighter hopes of better times;
Make peoples wise and nations free,
And link the whole earth silently.

And well we knew in days of yore,
The fire-breath bulls on Colchos' shore;
The fire-breath bulls with brazen heels,
Are yoked to common chariot-wheels;
And sounding o'er the land they go,
Though torrents rage and tempests blow;
Where they outstrip the fleetest wind,
A thousand men ride well behind;
And where the mart of commerce is,
They pant with loads of merchandise.
With breath of fire and brazen might,
They gleam by day and glow by night;

They blaze across the midnight downs,
Go snorting through the silent towns ;
They glitter o'er the sunny plain,
'Mid goodly lands of waving grain,
Through grassy vales of smiling peace,
Through wastes of slumbering silences !
Through busy towns they shriek and shrill,
Across the river, through the hill;
And wedding hearts by many a tie,
They link the whole land silently.

Where once the thunderbolt of Jove,
That through Mount Pelion's bosom clove,
Was forged within the Cyclops' den,
The Cyclops now are brawny men,
All working in the world's broad day ;
            And lo ! their lightning
            Now is brightening
The earth where once it spread dismay.
Its silent stream of sleeping fire
Is throbbing o'er a world-wide lyre,
Responding to the touch as truly
   As harp-strings to the player's hand ;
Words of love from utmost Thule
   Fall on ears on India's strand ;

The tidings which, some mother listening
　　For some lone ship of the sea,
Hears while her fond eyes are glistening—
　　Hope fulfilled in melody.
Tidings which some love-sick maiden
　　Prays some angel's wing to bear !
When her heart is overladen,
　　They drop in whispers through the air ;
The far away, and yet the dearer—
　　Though loving hands be far away,
Loving hearts are drawing nearer,
　　Drawing nearer every day.
One brother greets the morning sun,
　　　　And one the setting,
　　　　Unforgetting
Days when all their ways were one,
When one bright day-dawn looked upon
Their two bright faces, fresh and fair,
And glowing in the morning air !
Soft voices from the far-off home
　　Are whispering in the loved one's ear ;
And tones of hope and gladness come,
　　From far away, that home to cheer.
The words as sweet as maiden's lay
Are rushing round the earth alway;

In light along the wondrous wire,
The spirit-voices' silent choir,
The sweetest words that e'er were sung,
The sweetest harp that e'er was strung,
That wakes to notes of tenderness,
Of weal, of woe, of balm, and bliss,
Of hope and joy, of faith and love,
Of all that human hearts can move ;
And working aye by night and day,
It links the near and far away,—
It links the ages in their prime
With dreams of earth's young morning time,
Over hills and through the sea,
Linking the whole earth silently.

DAPHNE.

" Nondum laurus erat ; longoque descentia crine
Tempora cingebat de qualibet arbore Phœbus."
—OVID.

As yet the laurel did not exist; and Phœbus used to bind his temples, graceful with flowing locks, with leaves of any tree.

BEFORE Larissa's towers of fame
    Were founded by the old Pelasgic race ;
Or Hellene with his wanderers came
    From the rude lands of Thrace ;

Or lofty Gonnus' watchful city saw
    The beauty of Olympian Tempe's smile ;
Or sea-born Athos overawe
    The Sintians' far-off Isle :

Before the dawn of the heroic day
    That filled the ancient world with warrior deeds ;
Before the mountain Lapithæ
    Bestrode Thessalian steeds :

The river-god Peneus ruled the plain,
  And none was King in Thessaly save he;
From Orthys to Olympus owned his reign,
  From Pindus to the sea.

A grand old god, majestical and grey,
  He had one little child, and only one;
More beautiful—like some sweet summer day—
  Than aught she looked upon.

When she went dancing through the wilderness,
  When she went sparkling o'er the golden sand,
The little maiden, Daphne, was
  A radiance in the land.

Her eyes were like two fountains of delight,
  Where woodland sunbeams slumber all day
      through;
Two violets of Elysium, bright
  With the Elysian dew.

Her lips were like the first ambrosial kiss
  That tranced young Time at Love's celestial birth,
When loveliness with loveliness
  First met upon the earth.

Upon her cheeks two blushes had their home,
  Like Aphrodite's glowing through her hair,
When she rose sparkling from the pearly foam,
  Unconsciously fair.

The loving winds bore up her locks behind her,
  The golden curls that round the fillet throng;
Like sunbeams gleamed her limbs, so white and slender,
  The long green grass among.

Her songs were like a lute among the trees;
  And every creature listened to her voice,
And followed her, and bent it low to please—
  And she made all rejoice :

The snow-white blossom of the dark-green wood,
  The flower for which the land its leaves put on,
For which the trees in silent homage stood,
  For which the summer shone.

But through the woods there went a wandering lyre,
  Unseen the minstrel, and unsought the song;
It seemed as if Dodona's sylvan choir
  Lay all her paths along.

The grand old trees that curtained all the way
   Seemed filled with music, and from bush and brake
There came the same sweet lay
   Of love for her sweet sake.

And through the joyous light of summer morns
   It wove a thread of gladness all its own ;
She heard no more the satyrs' silvan horns,
   For her at evening blown.

And with her finger at her lip she listened,
   With upturned cheek, delighted yet afraid,
While tears of rapture on her eyelids glistened—
   " It is a god," she said.

" It is the God of Song himself, I know,
   And I am but a simple woodland maid ;
And yet I listen to him all day through—
   He cannot know," she said.

And she would run and seek her crystal hall,
   And nestle on the bosom of her sire ;
But never told the grey old king at all
   About the wandering lyre.

But one sad day a wounded hart rushed past her,
    Reddening the green grass with life's ebbing tide;
Though fast it ran, its life's red blood ran faster
    From its poor wounded side.

And by the warm red track the maiden traced it,
    When bent its light limbs like a broken wand;
And when the weeping maid caressed it,
    It kissed her gracious hand.

Who comes?   Ah, Daphne! that poor bleeding hart
    Hath chained thine eyes, sweet one.   They do
        not see
The god that loves thee; lonely as thou art,
    Fair child, arise and flee.

His royal step was light, his white limbs gleam
    Like marble: in his hand the silver bow
That slew the Python flashes beam on beam
    At every step even where no sun doth glow.

All round his head his locks in clusters flow,
    And scatter fragrance on the breathless winds,
That lift them like a radiance round his brow
    Which the bright cincture binds,

And let them on his stately shoulders fall,
   And on the golden clamys floating free ;
For never trod Olympian hall
   A god so fair as he.

He stood a moment with his lips apart,
   And strange sweet eyes, too bright to tell their hue ;
While Daphne, kneeling by the bleeding hart,
   No other presence knew,

Until the crackling twigs gave swift alarm :
   She rose all pale, till blushing wonder shed
A transient glow upon her lovely form ;
   And fleet as light she fled.

The two white forms rushed lightly through the glade,
   Flashed through the thicket, past the brown old trees ;
Brightness in sunshine, whiteness in the shade,
   And fleeter than the breeze.

" Stay, Daphne, stay, and be my woodland bride ! "
   The God exclaimed ; but Daphne would not hear ;
And through the trees she saw her native tide
   In the white sunshine near.

And from her lips there broke a sad long cry:
  " O father, help me ! " cried the breathless maid.
Then rose the grand old river, surging high
    Upon its pebbly bed.

Far up the vale her father's watery team
    Shook wildly in the air their tawny manes,
Their curvèd limbs strike out with sudden gleam
    As they rush down the plains.

Alas, alas, too late !   The panther's spring
    That of the suckling kid bereaves its dam,
The last swoop of the eagle's wing
    Down on the bleating lamb,

The long light bound that brought him to her side—
    He cried in joy, and clasped her in his arms,
" Now, Daphne, thou wilt be my woodland bride,
    Clad in immortal charms."

" Oh, let me go, great Phœbus ! " cried the child ;
    " O father, help me !   Is there no one nigh ? "
And the long wail broke through the silent wild—
    " O father, let me die ! "

And scarce within her heart sweet hope was dead,
   Her last sad prayer her lips had scarcely passed,
And scarce around the milk-white maid
   The God's bright arms were cast;

When life's last throb her spotless bosom heaves,
   And her sweet eyes were dimmed with their last tear;
And in the depths of laurel-leaves
   He saw her disappear.

Thus trembling still, as with her life's last quiver,
   A dark-green tree its glossy branches spread,
And o'er the mournful river
   It drooped its mournful head.

Then rustled through the woods one long sad sigh,
   As the repentant God stood weeping there;
And wilder still the childless agony
   Of her old sire's despair,

Who came too late to save, but not to see
   Her woeful fate—his ever lovely child.
" Away !" he cried, " and leave this spot to me,
   Like Daphne, undefiled.

"I am a God immortal, even as thou,
　　But thou hast made me childless evermore :
Leave me to nurse her with my sorrow now,
　　As my love heretofore."

"Forgive me, sire," the weeping God replied,
　　"And let me mourn with thee.　While ages flow,
My home shall be by her loved father's side,
　　Her leaves shall crown my brow ;

"Shall to the last of days be nobly worn,
　　As glorious as the diadem of kings ;
Shall wreathe the lyre, the patriot sword adorn,
　　The first of priceless things ;

"Make all but gods of men upon the earth ;
　　Filling grand anthems through the unborn days ;
With green old glory branching freely forth
　　To universal praise ;

"The meed of virtue and the crown of song,
　　That never eye of man shall see unmoved,
To tell the world the virtue and the wrong
　　Of Daphne the Beloved."

THE CONQUEST OF BACCHUS.

A LAY OF AN OLD GREEK VASE.

[IN the following poem the writer has departed no doubt from the more veracious chronicles of the gods, and the more generally received dogmas of the old Greek faiths. There is no word in classic story of an interview between Bacchus and Apollo, when the latter tended the flocks of King Admetus during his seven years' exile from Olympus, for killing the Cyclops. In fact, according to the more esoteric doctrines of the old mythological divines, Apollo and Bacchus are merely different manifestations of the same deity. Thus there is something like a heresy in ascribing to any influence of Apollo the agricultural results of the mysterious union of Bacchus and Ceres, although some may see in it

" The symbols of a larger sense,"

even according to mythological principles. Moreover, there is no doubt that the jealous Athenians would have warmly resented any attempt to represent Apollo as interfering in the special department of their tutelar deity, Pallas. Upon the whole, however, the old doctors of myth-

ology were very liberal in their views ; and, provided one
spoke respectfully of the Olympic conclave conjointly
and severally, they took little offence at the conduct,
humours, and peculiarities ascribed to them. The following poem is intended to represent the two phases in
the career of Dionysus,—viz., the frolicsome wine-god,
wild with the first joy of the grape, and roaming over
the world to establish his divinity—with wild beasts,
satyrs, and frantic mœnads in his train—till, either sub-
dued by some softer influence, or educated by experience,
he settled down into a gentlemanly god, and carrying his
experiments beyond the wine-vat into the virgin soil,
became the parent of Agriculture. If more general ideas
be sought, they will be found in the ordinary development
of man's life, and in the conquest of the sensual by the
spiritual, and that reunion of the spiritual with the
sensuous, which constitutes Art to ordinary apprehen-
sions.]

AN old Greek cup for old Greek wine,
That many an age has left unbroken,
And Time and Art made half divine !
Its mystic story, long unspoken,
> Seems to tell
> Some lesson well ;
Ivy-leaves and laurel twine
Round its lips—a pleasant token ;
Mirth and wisdom meetly join.

And once perchance this old Greek vase *
Has fired Panathenaic victors,
When filled with Pallas' oil of praise,—
The pride of potters and depictors.
　　　It brings the faces,
　　　Brings the graces,
Of the old, old years, and ways,
More clearly back than learned lectures,
All in the light of the old Greek days.

The dithyrambic chorus rings
Down from Pelion's piny mountain ;
Where Cithæron's forest flings
Deepest shades by Dirce's fountain,
　　　Rings the Evoe,
　　　Evoe ! Evoe !
Wake the dithyrambic strings,
From Bacchic Lydia's flowery mountain, †
And Pieria's woodland springs.

* At the greater or quinquennial Panathenaic games the principal
prizes consisted of vases containing oil from the sacred olives of the
Acropolis.　There, likewise, the potters of the street called Kerami-
cus, a highly-esteemed class of artists in those days, exhibited their
finest works.

† "The flowery Tmolus," as Euripides calls it, where Bacchus
was nursed.　As Lydia was the scene of the wine-god's infancy, the
other allusions to that somewhat pleasure-loving region may be left
to most people without further explanation.

Through forests green, with garlands gay,

His spotted panthers lightly guiding,

Giving earth a holiday,

And care and common things avoiding,

  He sweeps along,

  With shout and song,

The youthful God in glory riding,

Beauty brightening all the way,

And rosy Joy before him gliding.

Raise aloud the Lydian song,

Where Youth and Beauty tread the measure;

Raise aloud the Lydian song,

Where hearts, like wine-cups, brim with pleasure;

  Brimming o'er,

  By board and bower,

'Neath myrtle-boughs and skies of azure;

Raise aloud the Lydian song,

For youth is more than golden treasure.

With clustering grapes and flowing hair,

The radiant mazes lightly threading,

Hoary Time and all his care,

With kingly laughter all unheeding—

On they go,

Where roses blow,

Where wine-cups flow,

And love is leading,

Till they reach the valleys fair,

Where King Admetus' herds are feeding.

O the laughter ! O the song !

O the ivy ! O the laurel !

There they listen all day long,

A silent rapture, gathering o'er all ;

Hearts all listening,

Eyes all glistening,

As with careless grace they wore all,

O'er their snowy shoulders flung,

Their ivy crowns, and garlands floral.

Raise the song to higher themes,

Strike the lyre to louder numbers ;

Lydian measures lapt their dreams,

Delphic fires have burst their slumbers ;

    Burst the cloud,

    And burst the shroud—

Burst the cloud that beauty cumbers :

Psyche's moth in glory beams

Above its cerements of slumbers.

A shepherd touched the golden strings

To tones that woke the muses' wonder,

Sang the joy of olden things,

Outmurmured love, outrolled the thunder ;

    Griefs as deep

    As eyes could weep,

He sang—and drew, with accents tender,

Angels down, on folden wings ;

Made one of the hearts most wide asunder.

The herdsmen crowd from all the plain,
The satyrs leave their leafy cover—
Nymphs of Dian's sylvan train,
Beneath the forest-fringes hover;

>> Every hearer
>> Drawing nearer,

Listening to the wondrous strain,
Till their wild sweet eyes run over
Amber light and holy rain.

A newer beauty spread abroad,
More leafy fair the forest growing—
A brighter green o'ershed the sod,
More brightly sweetest blossoms blowing;

>> At every tone
>> The sunbeams shone

More fair—and men, in rapture glowing,
Kneel all around the minstrel god,
Their spirits with his anthems flowing.

G

And brighter still the glory grew;

The wine-god dropt his sparkling chalice:

Each wild Bacchante's eyes dropt dew,

As sweet as flowers by Lydian Halys;

  All bow before

  Such tones of power

As ne'er Tyrrhennian trumpet blew,

Nor were awoke when Indian valleys

Heard the Panic Eilleleu.

The old Ægean's sullen roar

Is hushed, as from Olympus' zenith,

Down the soft Thessalian shore

A voice proclaims—Apollo reigneth!

  And they wear all

  Wreaths of laurel,

Not an ivy crown remaineth;

Bacchus' lays are alien lore,

His purple light of glory waneth.

Waneth? no! a nobler morn
Its lustrous light is round him shedding;.
Springs the olive, sprouts the corn,
Where his rosy foot is treading.
> Ever strewing,
> Overflowing
Blessings, over lands forlorn,
Peace and plenty round him spreading,
Rich as Amalthea's horn.

Then raise again the Lydian song
To Phœbus' lyre in nobler measures;
The shrilling syrinx, silent long,
Faintly pleads for Bacchic pleasures.
> Lo! the God
> Has blessed the sod;
Lo! the thyrsus teems with treasures;
> While they wear all
> Wreaths of laurel—
Ivy glints the leaves among,
Wisdom o'er all, wine to cheer all—
Raise again the Lydian song.

For lo ! the songs of forest-trees
Are all of beauty and abundance ;
In every rustling autumn breeze
Are songs of fertile fields' redundance ;
As boyhood bright,
So fleet of flight,
Throws back its light of long-gone glees,
O'er manhood's heart with soft resplendence
Bacchus cometh back to please.

Bacchus, beautiful and young,
Come back to labour late and early,
Conquered by the glorious song
That great Apollo sings so yarely !
And through all his
Hills and valleys
Breaks the light of beauty fairly—
Breaks the hymn from every tongue,
And rings through all the woodlands clearly.

The laurels, where young Daphne died,
Grow green beside her parent river;
The dews of Pindus swell the tide,
And keep them fresh and green for ever—
      The greener still,
      By stream and hill,
That laurelled song is silent never,
That love and joy go side by side,
And mirth and wisdom seldom sever.

Then raise the dithyrambic song;
While higher thoughts bring higher pleasures,
Pray thee, count it nothing wrong,
If both these Gods should mix their measures.
      Let Bacchus follow
      Young Apollo,
Strewing round him rural treasures,
      While they wear all
      Wreaths of laurel,
Ivy sprigs the leaves among,
Through nobler aims like lighter pleasures,
Twine again the lightsome song.

THE ROSE-A-LYNN.

PART I.

THE white, white rose, and the yellow whin,
Are all the flowers that grow at Lynn :
The rose for one fair Rose's fate,
The whin for a house made desolate.
The fields are rich, the woodland heaves
The billowy breast of its sea of leaves,
But the raven croaks on the ruined wall,
The she-fox whelps are in the hall ;
The fields were sown, and left unshorn
Their murmuring lands of yellow corn :
And who shall find me kith or kin
Of all the brave old lords of Lynn?

The sun shone down on no such pair
As our good lord and lady fair,
When in the pomp of princely state
The Court rode down the Canongate ;

Or when the knights rode at the ring,
· At castled Stirling with the king;
Or when in their own dales more blest
They rode alone, with hawk on wrist.
And brave and fair, the legend tells,
Were matched like the goshawk's Milan bells.

But swords that kept their master's trust
Had then but little time to rust,
And with his peers the Lord of Lynn
Had name to make and fame to win.
The sound of his falcon-bells is still,
The bay of his hound on the silent hill;
The grey old grandsires shear the corn,
The maidens bind the sheaves and mourn.
And young and old, and rich and poor,
Their hearts are on the Borough Muir,
Where in the king's array of war
Their lord and his retainers are.

And one sweet child at her mother's knee,
As fairly fair as child could be—
A bud beside the parent rose,
Both bathed in dew, at evening close,
Was all the joy that he left at Lynn
To the Heart that brought his summer in.

Alas and woe that day of pain,
When Scotland bled at every vein !
When round the foot of Flodden hill,
And through the fords of mossy Till,
Lay rank on rank all rusty red,
The faithful phalanx of the dead.
Ah, tears ! alas that day of fate !
  Ah, tears ! alas that night of woe !
Alas for hearts made desolate !
  Whose tears shall never cease to flow.

Alas the hope—it faded fast—
That her lost lord might come at last !
Might still come home,—might live and be
In England in captivity,
And yet come home some rosy morn,
To wake his woodlands now forlorn.

Such clouded hopes but seldom smiled ;
  But in their pale and wintry gleam
She fondly clasped her sweet maid-child,
  And whispered her delusive dream.
And noon and night she went to pray,
Down in the chapel old and grey,
That since King Malcolm's days had stood
Within the shadow of the wood :

And organ peal and holy hymn
  Rose sadly sweet, till every tree,
All silent in the twilight dim,
  Seemed hushed in some sweet reverie.

But whence that cry, from faint to wild—
"Where is my child, my darling child?
Good father, speak!   But now, but here,
She stood by my side, so very near,
I heard her accents low and sweet,
As she sang the hymn; and her little feet
Went whispering over the stony floor.
She is scarcely out at the chapel door.
Where is my child?   Good father, tell!
Good sacrist, ring the chapel bell!"

They rang it loud, they rang it long;
They gathered in a wondering throng
Of peasants, up and down the glen,
And all the castle serving-men.
'Twas part in wonder, part in fear,
And part it was the news to hear,
And part because the country-side
With bonfires blazed for Hallow-tide.

It was the night to fairies free,
  When warlocks ride the raid of sin,
And only love and loyalty
  Could face the gloomy woods of Lynn.
But even love had little cheer
That night of all nights of the year.
So forth they fared all true and kind,
But scarcely dared to speak their mind :
St Mary, save our lady lass,
On this dark eve of Hallowmas !
And still the bell rang loud and well,
Up through the wood with long sweet swell ;
And still the sound rolled o'er the ground ;
The bell will ring till the child be found.

They searched the wood, in hope and fear,
As startled as the startled deer ;
Then torches gleamed from tree to tree,
And the old bell kept them in company.
They said, " Our search is vain, 'tis true,
But we will do what men may do."
And good true men and fearless, they
Had never shunned the battle-day !
But they at once were strong and weak ;
  They sained themselves the way to clear,

From brow to breast, from cheek to cheek,
  That night of all nights of the year.

Alas! 'twas vain; the morrow morn
Still found the mother lone and lorn.
Alas! 'twas vain; the days passed on,
The flickering ray of hope was gone.
But whether, in their moonlight raid,
The fairies stole the little maid;
Or whether ruder robber hand
Had ta'en at once the life and land,
All hope grew dark amid the dool
Of widowed Scotland's darkest Yule,
And passed away the Light of Lynn,
That brought her young lord's summer in.

PART II.

The chain of days flows link on link,
And the change is all in ourselves, I think;
The years in their golden circles flow,
But the mist is on those of long ago.
The primrose of the last March morn
  Was the flower of a thousand springs;
And the child of a thousand years is born
  To the same old ways of things.

The change is all in the cunning hand,
And the wider grasp of man's command,
And the keener sight of clearer eyes,
That have banished the strange old mysteries ;
But the same sweet hopes and the same sad fears,
    The old, old love, and the old, old woe,
Look up through the light of all the years,
    With the mist on the years of long ago.

And through the wood went a laughing band
Of blithe little maidens hand in hand ;
They danced and sang through the woodland way,
Like the blithe little maids of yesterday.
They sang sweet, sweet, on the blaeberry knowes,
    Till their red, red lips were blue,
And they twined about their fair young brows
    The fairest flowers that grew.

They passed the chapel old and grey,
Where the Light of Lynn had died away :
And a white old monk looked out in the sun,
And he blessed the children one by one.
And sweetly rang their songs of glee,
    Through the dark-green woodland gloom,
Till a little maid came to a fair rose-tree,
    With a single rose in bloom.

A milk-white rose far more than fair,
Its fragrance told its presence there;
And as she kissed it like a child,
It gleamed and glowed as if it smiled.
A rose of such sweet gracious white
　　Had ne'er been seen in all the land;
She touched it, and a golden light
　　Seemed glimmering on her hand.

She plucked the rose, as a little maid will,
And it blossomed anew and fairer still.
Again and again, and could it be true?
As fast as she plucked them they blossomed anew.
It was wondrous fair in its glossy robe,
　　Which the flowers came peeping through;
Each white, white, white, like a pearl globe
　　Of light and crystal dew.

The children gazed in fond surprise,
With a strange sweet awe in their tremulous eyes;
Though deep was their wonder and dreary the spot,
The flower was so fair they feared it not.
And they brought the monk from chapel grey
　　To the spot where the white rose grew;
And aye as they took the roses away,
　　They budded and blossomed anew.

The tale was told in hall and hut,
At the Sunday mass and the shooting butt;
And the young and old went forth to see
The snow-white rose in its mystery.
It was whiter and fairer than all its kind,
   More bountiful its store;
Like a thing that the angels had left behind,
   In the saintly days of yore.

Forth went the churchmen to sain the wood,
With book and bell and holy rood:
But like dew of the morning on flower and spray
The drops of the holy water lay.
The woodman went with axe and spade,
   At the Lord of Lynn's command,
" But the iron was never forged," he said,
   "That will root that rose from the land."

And far and near the pilgrims came,
To see this flower of wondrous fame;
There came the sick, there came the sound,
And the woodland dell was holy ground.
At market, mass, and holiday,
   The same strange tidings ran,
That a new-blown flower from its fragrant spray
   Would give life to a dying man.

It seemed so pure from earth and sin,
They called it the saintly Rose-a-Lynn,
As it hung its head with a piteous grace,
Like a child forlorn in a wilderness.
It was pearl white, it was dewy bright,
   It was meek as a veilèd nun ;
And it glowed like the flakes of virgin light,
  · In the land of the morning sun.

PART III.

Alas ! when all the country wide
Is heavy of heart at Lammas-tide;
When summer brings not summer cheer,
Nor lifts the shadow from the year,
Nor feeds the kine, nor fills the corn,
   Nor lights with hope a bluer sky ;
But all the mass of men are born
   To sunken cheek and leaden eye :

When horses carried clanking steel
Instead of sacks of malt and meal;
When rusty blade and ragged cloak
Caused daily fear to honest folk ;

When bishops' crooks were changed to swords,
　　And baby brows were crowned ;
And wife and child to Scottish lords
　　Were less than horse and hound :

When Borthwick, Liddel, Esk, and Ouse,
Saw Dacre burn a thousand ploughs
From Clyde to Nith, from Forth to Tweed—
Who wanted pith must trust to speed ;
When Dee and Deveron, Tay and Forth,
　　Were reived by red-shank caterans,
And robber chiefs through all the north
　　Were all the law of lawless clans :

When yeomen left their farming gear
For rusty splent and three-eln spear ;
To hinds their oxen, plough, and gad,
And their flocks to a piping shepherd lad ;
Till they waxed poor and the burghers rich,
　　And filled with pride to that degree,
That the best or worst I wot not which,
　　Their pride or the yeoman's poverty:

When the vicar's teinds and baron's mail
Left little but rags and water-kail ;

And curses were sold for a year to come,
And pardons hawked at the tuck of drum ;
" And the only cure," said the priestly saints,
    " That can purge our Scottish soil,
Is a blaze of Dutch New Testaments
    For the Lollard louns of Kyle."

But the autumn noon in a haze of gold
Lay hushed like a dream of the days of old,
The solemn gloom and the dusky glow
Of the old oak-woods of long ago.
The sun was as bright, the world as fair,
    As if Earth knew neither grief nor sin ;
And the people came from far and near
    To see the Rose-a-Lynn.

The thrifty burgher locked his till,
And came in his holiday tunikil ;
The yeomen came from their cold wet farms
In leathern coats like men-at-arms ;
And all for the saintly rose, said they,
    Which works such wonders through the land ;
And every man looked tenderly
    On the white rose in his hand.

H

The dames came according to their degree
In russet and fine French crammasie,
With silken cloak with cristy grey,
Beside the homeliest rokelay ;
And maidens came in scarlet hoods
   And kirtles green and blue :
And sheen and shadow through the woods
   With sprightly lads enow.

And begging monks, with dusty knee,
And many a benedicite ;
And red-shanks, with their heather hair,
And deerskin shoon and legs half-bare ;
And Dusty-feet,* with heavy packs,
   Who seldom ventured up the glen
To seek a scanty crop of placks
   Within the bounds of broken men.

And it's all for the Rose-a-Lynn, said they,
The flower of hope in a hopeless day,
The saintly rose in its simple grace,
The pure white thing of the wilderness—
So fair in its snow-white purity,
   That it stands in the world alone,
Like the ruby flower of the golden tree
   In the lands of Prester John.

* The old name for a wandering merchant.

Part IV.

It was the time when hound and horn
For matin bells awoke the morn ;
When courtiers changed their silken suits
For Kendal coats and buckskin boots.
It was the merry hunting time
   For the roebuck and the stag ;
From Lammas-tide till Michaelmas rime .
   Lay white on holt and hag.

The Lord of Lynn was as strange a sight
To his own broad lands as the sun at night ;
And his lady held them in disdain,
And harried them through her chamberlain.
But he was one of Angus' men,
   And he came with a gallant company,
When Douglas ruled the land again
   . In spite of the Queen and Albany.

They spent in hunting all the day,
The night they spent in their deraye :
And little recked though Angus' lot
Should fail when Falkland's bolts were shot.

The knights went forth with horn and hound,
　The dames with palfreys fair;
While Milan bells of silver sound
　With sweetness filled the air.

The dames gave music to their glee;
The knights, to show their forestry,
Their horns in gay contention wound
To every moot that they could sound.
The moot for a Bevy of Roes, they cry,
　As they pass the burgher maidens by;
And loud and clear from the mellow horn
　Came the sweetest notes of an autumn morn.
For the dames—the moot for a Cackle of Geese;
　For the youths—a Sound of Swine;
But the moots to them were meaningless,
　And they deemed the music fine.

But merry laugh and gleeful din
Were all unheard by the Lord of Lynn;
They were lost in the organ's solemn swell,
And the sound of the old appealing bell.
For twelve long years that awful psalm
　He had heard on land and sea;
That pealing bell, in storm and calm,
　Had called him home to his destiny.

He banned the bell, but still it rang ;
It filled his ear with sullen clang :
And still it rang though liquid hot—
It had passed through Arran's smelting-pot.
It rang as it rang that night of fear
  When deer-fleet feet sped o'er the grass ;
That night of all nights of the year,
  The death-dark eve of Hallowmas.

Away he rushed, but still the sound
With iron tongue rolled o'er the ground ;
While nameless terrors all unheard
Stood foaming on his tawny beard :
"Go, pitch those organ-pipes to hell ; "
  " There is no organ there."
" My horse to him who sends that bell
  In fragments through the air."

"There is no bell," his squires reply :
"God's blood ! the idiot scullions lie !"
A bell ! ah, true ! a passing-bell,
A spirit-bell that rang the knell
Of him to whom it rang in vain
  Those ghostly tones so fraught with woe,
From which no shrift his soul can sain
  From the dead old days of long ago.

With trembling lip and flattened ears,
The good horse shared his master's fears;
He felt the rider's shuddering limb,
And all his terror passed to him.
And off they rushed, and through the dell
    The blast of green-clad hunters broke;
And fast the Baron's curses fell
    Among the crowd of common folk—

Both fast and fierce.   He had the craft
To hide his fears in words of wrath;
While with his boar-spear's ashen haft
He cleared the crowded bridle-path.
But what was ghostly organ-boom,
    Or phantom bells that filled the air,
To that white rose of wonder-bloom,
    And there—of all creation there?

There, in the shade of rock and pine,
Where woodbine and ivy trail and twine—
Where the dusky light of broken rays
Shed round the glow of a golden haze—
The white rose shone like a silver star,
    Like a spirit robed in mystery,
With its pearl bloom and its silk symar,
    And the light of its saintly purity.

The sun might set, and still as white
It shone in beauty all the night;
The sun might gild its lonely lot,
It gave more beauty than it got.
It seemed a thing of a stranger clime,
　　That had flowered to hymns of praise;
A remnant of some holier time,
　　Of the immemorial days.

The rain might fall, the wind might blow
The winter hurricane of snow:
It sat like a maid in a silken snood,
In a breathless calm in the windy wood.
It was calm as light, it was pure as dew,
　　And the fragrance that round it hung
Was the fragrance of Eden where first it grew,
　　When the virgin world was young.

And whether it had power to move,
To wonder most, or most to love,
I may not say; so beautiful,
So wonderful, so pitiful,
That one could almost love and weep,
　　And one could almost kneel and pray;
It brought to mind the things that keep
　　The fragrance of the heavens alway.

And round and round sat carle and knave,
And maiden gay and matron grave,
All in the shade of the soft greenwood,
In the pleasant sense of neighbourhood—
The bond that links both high and low,
　　Outside the closer tie of blood,
Which double hearts can never know,—
　　The pleasant sense of neighbourhood.

And hands as rough as hands could be,
They plucked the rose right tenderly ;
And a new flower filled its sister's place,
In still more gracious loveliness.
In awe they saw in pearl rings
　　The petals silently unfold,
And rise through the spray like living things,
　　To the touch of young and old.

A young knight led my Lady in ;
Come, see your sister, the Rose-a-Lynn,
The fairest flower on bush or tree,
And the fairest flower in the land, said he.
He cut a rose with his hunting-knife,
　　And placed it in her hand.
" St Mary ! " she cried, " the thing has life,
　　It has come from Fairyland."

And still anew the roses grew
From bud to bloom, and still anew
They opened up their blossoms white,
In the crystal glow of their own sweet light.
And aye they culled with words of praise,
    And it blossomed ere they wist,
In the dewy light of a sapphire blaze,
    Half quenched in silver mist.

" My Lord is sick," said the grey old monk,
" His cheek is pale and his eye is sunk ;
A single bud from the Rose-a-Lynn,
Will bring the life-blood back to the skin."
" Lo here, my Lord ! lo there, my Lord !"
    Cried knight and squire, and plucked the spray;
" My halidome ! not Jonah's gourd
    Flowered half so fast by Nineveh."

And still the flowers came silently,
Came solemnly, came bounteously,
With a rarer light and a sweeter grace,
And a more exceeding loveliness.
" A witch-flower cursèd root and branch,
    Bring pine and pitch, the woods are mine !"
" A rose that doth thy visage blanch,
    Will flower through blazing pitch and pine."

" What recreant shaveling have we here ? "
The Baron cried, 'twixt wrath and fear,
And bent him low to his saddle-bow,
While the brown beads sat on his clay-cold brow :
He bent him low the rose to clutch ;
   When shriek on shriek rang through the wood,
As the saintly flower fell down at his touch,
   In a purple mist and a pool of blood.

Back started dame and cavalier ;
The folk behind crowd still more near ;
While rose the fierce perturbent cry—
" I have found thee, O mine enemy ! "
And tawny lord and grey-haired monk
   Stood face to face, if so might be,
Where one from every gazer shrunk,
   And one stood upright as a tree.

And through the wood still rang the cry,
" I have found thee, O mine enemy ! "
Away, away, and all away,
The saintly rose and silken spray ;
While o'er the red and misty ground,
   Where all the wondrous record lies,
Like blood-streaked spear-points gather round
   The circle of accusing eyes.

And still they gather round the scene,
Where so much loveliness had been,
The mystery of beauty so
Lost in the mystery of woe,
That every heart took up the wrong,
   And every tongue took up the cry,
In one low wail from old and young,
   "I have found thee, O mine enemy!"

" Begone, thou Cain, my woes may tell,
But thine is woe unspeakable,"
The churchman said ; and stern and low
Fell word on word like blow on blow.
He saw not here, he saw not there,
   The awe-struck men before him pass ;
He saw the thing that was so fair,
   He saw the blood upon the grass.

" He slew them both, so loved by me ;
Why slew he not the hapless three ?
He found me in that precious ring
Of broken jewels, round their king.
The wounded chief of all his race
   He doomed in secret bonds to lie
These twelve long years.   Now face to face
   I have found thee, O mine enemy!"

And, lo ! they saw the red ooze pass
Away in the sun from the misty grass ;
And a fountain pure as the morning dew
Burst out of the sod where the white rose grew ;
And it flows and flows in sun and shade,
    A mercy wrought.of woe and sin :
And it will flow when we are dead,
    Where flowered the saintly Rose-a-Lynn.

KING SIGURD, THE CRUSADER.

A NORSE SAGA.

THE minster-bells from morning light
　　With solemn sweetness rang;
The trumpet-call of every night
　　Gave forth its brazen clang.

And friend with friend stood hand in hand,
　　And foes were friends that day,
When young King Sigurd left the land,
　　With the Knights of Norroway.

And maid and wife, as dear as life,
　　All beautiful and true,
Stood weeping there, like roses rare,
　　All drooping wet with dew:

And many a silent prayer was prayed,
 And many a heart was sore,
For love of wife, and love of maid,
 And fears of Nevermore.

And through the crowd, whose shouts were loud,
 While women wept with ruth,
Came the King, the young Crusader,
 In the beauty of his youth.

Scarce seventeen suns their summer light
 Upon his cheek had shed ;
And his yellow hair was golden bright
 As the crown upon his head.

He passed the loveliest of the land,
 The pride of many a hall,
And little maiden Hinda's hand
 He kissed before them all.

" I'm nameless but for Magnus' line,
 Unknown but for my crown,
I'll wed thee when its gold doth shine
 In the light of my renown."

He said, and then with all his men,
  He sailed through Agg'hrus' Bay, `
And King Sigurd, the Crusader,
  Was the King of Norroway.

———

There's manhood in the mountain land,
  There's freedom on the sea—
The might of heart that must command—
  The hearts that must be free.

And southward where the summers smile,
  Their gilded galleys dance ;
They feasted long in England's isle,
  And fought the knights of France.

Where'er the Red-Cross banner led
  Against the Moors of Spain,
Along the van the Sea-kings' blade
  Showered round its ruddy rain.

The iron tide of war they turned
  At Cintra and Seville ;
And many a Moorish widow mourned
  The fair-haired Norseman's steel.

As down the Scareberg's trembling void,
   Sweep ice-bound floods of snow;
As rolls the Maelstrom's deadly tide,
   From Mosky to Meroe;

So broke then war o'er land and sea,
   Where Paynim foe was found;
And the Corsairs of Brown Barbary
   They drove through Nörfa's * Sound.

Red rolled the wave o'er many a grave
   On Formentura's shore,
With freedom to the Christian slave
   Who pulled the pirate's oar;

And green Minorca's captives free,
   Round young King Sigurd cling;
And Roger, Earl of Sicily,
   He crowned and made a king.

In many a tongue the praise was sung,
   In many a minstrel's lay,
Of King Sigurd, the Crusader,
   And the Knights of Norroway.

----

* The Straits of Gibraltar, so called from the first Scandinavian
seaman who passed them.

When first in holy Palestine,
  Their pilgrim feet they set,
They knelt and kissed that land divine
  Which God's own blood had wet.

They rode like men for war arrayed,
  These northern Sea-kings all;
And all their way King Baldwin spread,
  With purple and with pall.

" Such pomp our state but seldom brooks;
  Our arms are all our store;
But look ye as your leader looks,—
  Look ever on before!"

And thus they trod, where'er they rode,
  O'er royal robes, that lay
Like dust beneath King Sigurd's feet,
  And the Knights of Norroway.

King Baldwin sought with treasure brought
  To try their strength once more;
They looked as though they saw it not—
  Looked ever on before.

I

"Your gold give to yon pilgrim band,"
  The young King Sigurd said;
"He wants not wealth by sea or land
  Who wears the Norseman's blade."

Then came they where stood maidens fair
  In richest raiment dressed,
Whose loveliness, King Baldwin sware,
  Would thaw Pope Sergius' breast.

"See, over them, Jerusalem,
  All desolate this day!"
Said King Sigurd, the Crusader,
  To the Knights of Norroway.

"See, over them, Jerusalem,
  And far, and farther o'er,
Where maid and wife, as dear as life,
  Are waiting on the shore!

"Let truth betide the Sea-king's bride,
  Whose breast is like the foam;
The maids of all the world beside
  Are not like those at home."

He raised his crown from off his head,
   But turned he not his eye;
As beauteous as a beauteous maid,
   As stately passed he by.

" These men are men," said Baldwin, then—
   " Are kings from head to heel;
To death, to life, to love and strife,
   As true as ice-brook steel;

" And blest the clime o'er all the earth,
   The land where'er it be,
The mothers all who gave them birth,
   These Norsemen of the sea!"

And long and well, as minstrels tell,
   They fought the Paynim foe;
And Acre's rock-built ramparts fell,
   Before the Norsemen's blow.

On Sidon's walls their banner flew
   Above the Crescent Star;
And every man the Sea-king knew
   Who led the Christian war.

The Red Cross shone on Askelon,
   And foremost all the day
Was the King, the young Crusader,
   With the Knights of Norroway.

And many a tongue the praises sung
   Of Sigurd and his band;
And the fame of grey old Norroway
   Grew great in every land.

Yet many a silent prayer was prayed,
   And many a heart was sore,
With love of wife and love of maid,—
   The looked-for Evermore.

And sweetly sang the summer gales,
   When westward went their prow;
And gaily shone their silken sails
   Round stormy Lindesnoe.

Their praise was sung, the bells were rung,
   And hearts were full and free;
And maid and wife, as dear as life,
   Were waiting by the sea.

Through smiles and tears, and loving cheers,
    And trumpet-notes of fame,
Came King Sigurd, the Crusader,—
    Like a conqueror he came.

There stood the noblest of the land,
    The pride of many a hall,
But lovely lady Hinda's hand
    He kissed before them all.

He said, while in her downcast eyes
    The tears of rapture glow,
And in her blush of sweet surprise
    The flowers of beauty blow,—.

" If we come back with fame as fair
    As we have kept our truth,
Then I may claim right well to wear
    The blossoms of thy youth.

" My knights have won the world's renown
    In many a deadly day;
But the light that gilds King Sigurd's crown,
    Is the love of Norroway."

THE TROUBADOUR.

" By sails and oars did Geoffry Rudel find
The death that he desired."—PETRARCH.

" Irat et dolent m'en partray,
  S'ieu non vey cet amour de luench,
  Et non sey qu'oura la veray,
  Car sont trop noutras terras luench."
              —*From the Provençal of* GEOFFRY RUDEI
                      in Sismondi.

" SHE's far away—
  She's far away ;
Alas ! my love is far away."
Twas thus that Geoffry Rudel sang,
  The minstrel prince of Blaye.

One lady's name,
One lady's fame,
He heard where'er crusader came.
The wandering palmer told her praise,
  And many an exile's prayer had she ;
Her beauty filled the minstrel's lays,
  And fired the Frankish chivalry.

They left the maids of Rhòdes to mourn,
  They left the lands they went to free,
And many a knight the cross had worn,
  To win the flower of Tripoli.
A princess of the western line—
  Of gentle Raymond of Toulou;
Her sires had fought in Palestine,
  Where'er Duke Godfrey's banner flew;
And now her name in love's sweet tone
  Was heard her father's shores along.
By field and stream and forest lone,
  In many a flood of song.

And thus one minstrel sadly sang,
As aye he swept his matchless lyre,
  The tale of passion as it sprang
Forth, burning from his heart of fire—
  " Oh ! happy birds for ever free *
To sing of love so light to mine
  That I must grieve o'er, silently.
The shepherds with their pipes do rove,
  The children on their tabors play,

---

* Extracts from Geoffry Rudel's poems, in which frequent allu-
sion is made to the distant object of his affections.

While I alone in sadness pine
   For her so loved, so far away.'
Thus sung the gallant troubadour
   That ruled the lands of Blaye.

And though his eye ne'er knew the bliss
   Of lingering o'er that loved one's face,
He sighed along the troubled wave
   That washed his own belovèd strand,
" It's oh, to be the meanest slave
   That waits by that fair lady's hand !
It's oh, to find a lowly grave,
   And lie within her land !
No more I'll wander, lorn and lone,
   The banks of my beloved Garonne ;
No more I'll walk this wild-wood shade ;
   The forest-flowers are dead to me ;
No home can be my home, sweet maid,
   Save thy fair town of Tripoli."

His lance was foremost in the lists,
   His lay within the lady's bower ;
But long in vain the fair Guienne
   Will mourn her absent troubadour ;
For o'er the ocean swelling wide,
   Now floats his melancholy lay ;

The rugged seamen weep beside,
   As still he sings—" She's far away."
His lyre so sweetly murmured on
   Where swept the waves like liquid gold ;
But wildly, boldly rung its tone,
   Where stormy waters roared and rolled.
And now triumphant hope it told—
   Now did it wail in wild despair ;
And now to gentler fancies mould
   Its tones upon the ocean air.

But sadder grew both lay and lyre,—
The minstrel's heart had lost its fire ;
   And as the long-sought lady's land
Arose before his languid eye,
   And ere his bark had touched the strand,
He knew that he had come to die.
   But still he sang in broken tones—
" Oh ! welcome death, when hope is dead ;
   The land will hold my mould'ring bones,
That this belovèd one doth tread."
   He gave the groves of his Garonne
   For a grave by lonely Lebanon :
And still his prayer was once to see
The peerless maid of Tripoli.

And lo ! ere death had closed his eye,
　　A beauteous vision met his view,
Such as the fervent ecstasy
　　Of inspiration never drew.
And well his heart the loved one knew—
　　His lonely dreams had cherished long,
When fancy half prophetic grew,
　　And showed the subject of his song.
The lady kissed his clay-cold brow,
　　And many a tear of sorrow shed ;
He gently smiled on her, and lo !
　　The minstrel's gallant spirit fled.
The voice of song was hushed in death ;
　　But she so loved when far away,
In sorrow drank thy dying breath,
　　Thou princely Troubadour of Blaye.
She said, while weeping by his side—
　　" No other heart hath earth like thine ;
And I will be thy widowed bride,
　　And wed thy memory to mine.
Adieu ! adieu ! ye glittering throng—
　　Ye joys that now no longer bless ;
No song is left like Rudel's song—
　　No love within the world like his."
And drooping as a willow-wand,
　　She's ta'en the circlet from her brow,

The rings from off her velvet hand,
    The bracelets from her arm of snow ;
And rich attire and princely halls
    She bartered for a convent's gloom,
Where, 'mid its sad and silent walls,
    She raised her minstrel lover's tomb :
And there in prayer long pined away
    Such beauty as men seldom see,
Till, by the Troubadour of Blaye,
    Was laid the Maid of Tripoli.

NOTE.—The story of Geoffry Rudel and the Princess of Tripoli is almost historical. According to M. de St Peluze it is told by writers who lived about their time, and received universal credence for two centuries.

The Tripoli referred to is not to be confounded with the African Tripoli in Barbary. It stands on the ruins of the three cities of Tyre, Sidon, and Aradus, and is consequently called the Triple City—in the modern Arabic form, Tarabulis. The ruins of the Castle of Count Raymond of Toulouse, built soon after the city was taken from the Saracens, in the twelfth century, are still to be seen on the bank of the river Kadisha, which intersects the city.

THE FLIGHT OF THE ABENCERRAGE.

THE Golden Cross is more than bright,
And more than dim the Crescent's light;
The blast from Christian trumpets borne,
Has drowned the mellow Moorish horn.
While round Grenada's leaguered walls
  The high heart proudly beats—
There's woe within her palace halls,
  There's wailing in her streets.

Her hills, where vines and olives spread,
Resound to many a foeman's tread;
Her groves lie crushed on every plain,
Beneath the feet of conquering Spain.
Field after field has seen the best
  Of her defenders fall,
And treachery has thinned the rest,
  And hope has left them all.

'Twas night—a night of grief and sorrow,
Sad presage of the coming morrow;
And strange dark tidings were afloat,
And every moment others brought:
When, hark! the sound of the warlike horn,
　　The tramp of crowding feet,
And murmurs swelling loud are borne
　　Along the sounding street.

Ho! is it men to man the wall?
Or is it Musa's battle-call?
A sudden sally, while the foe
Sleeps off his last night's wine? Ah, no!
Such eagle-swoops need stronger wings
　　Than bear our legions now.
Hark! loud and louder still it rings,
　　And loud the murmurs grow.

See, where the torches' lurid light
Flash red on many a Moorish knight.
But more than mailèd men are there.
Well may the sleepy households stare
On matron fair and maiden mild,
And many a tired and weeping child,
And many a peaceful citizen,
And Moorish priests, and serving-men!

They move like mourners of the dead,
  In silence and dismay:
No proud triumphal cavalcade,
  No festal band are they.

What chief is he whose trumpet-tongue
Through all their weeping ranks has rung?
They would not crowd thus closely round
A laggard at the gathering sound.
'Tis Musa of the eye of light,
  Far flashing like a star;
And his that plume of spotless white,
  That leads the Moorish war.

Grenada's bravest chieftain he,
Her trust in her extremity!
In silent wonder stands the chief;
He speaks in wonder and in grief—
Why ride the Abencerrages
  As in a shameful flight,
Where old, the young, their whole great race,
  Go cowering through the night?

The tempest-cloud, the lightning's flash,
The floods that chase the thunder-crash ;
·Their darkening brows, their eyes of fire,
The tears that mingle with their ire !
What has not Musa heard?   Our wrong?
Our fate in this dread night of woe,
Such as was never sung in song,
Nor told in tale of friend or foe?

To-night our chieftains feasted all
In the Alhambra's banquet-hall ;
Oh, black with curses be the hour
That gave them to the tyrant's power !
In faith they gave the bare right hand,
    Unhelmed was every brow ;
Behold us here, a bleeding band !
    Where are the mighty now?
The noblest of our ancient name
    Lie stiffening in their gore,
And Aben-Amar's sword of flame
    Will light our wars no more.

A woe-wrought monument of stone,
A very grief to look upon,
Stood Musa, while around him rise
His kindred's groans and oaths and cries.

And still he is my king, he said,
   That my best blood begrimes ;
My hand must shield his royal head,
   In follies or in crimes.

'Mid woes and woes, a thousand woes,
Grenada stands before her foes !
Shall we prove false for vengeance' sake ?
What though Grenada's flames ye slake
With her own blood, for vengeance shed ?
Such treachery would shame the dead.
It was not thus Cordova's host
   Fell slaughtered round her towers ;
It was not thus Toledo lost
   The Crescent of the Moors ;

Nor thus that the Nevadas saw
Your fathers fall in Murcia :
But step by step and side by side,
They victors fought, or vanquished died.
Though cursed by many a civil jar,
That made our foes the men they are,
They were not traitors : they ! ah, no !
   They died, and died amid their fame ;
But like Gehenna's endless woe,
   To them, to me, the traitor's shame.

Grenada Queen ! Grenada fair !
   Grenada glory of the land !
These were thy sons ! my brethren were !
   But thine is my right hand.
My father, mother, child, and wife—
   My kindred thou, my hope, my all—
With thee, for thee, to live is life,
   With thee, for thee, I fall ;
And lost amid thy tearful story
   Shall be my life, shall be my death—
No renegade to glory,
   To my home, or to my faith.

'Twas vain ! though tears where tears were strange
Fell fast, they could not quench revenge.
The mournful cavalcade moved on ;
And faithful Musa stood alone.
Alone ! the last of all his race ;
   Alone ! and face to face with fate ;
As scornful of the Christians' grace,
   As resolute as desolate.
He saw the white Alhambra lie
   Beneath the waning moon,
And through the narrow street pass by
   The crowd as if at noon.

K

He heard the gathering trumpet borne
  In from the Spanish posts,
And all the night and all the morn,
  The marshalling of hosts.
And all the night and all the morn
Was heard the clanging Moorish horn;
And long before the dawn of day
Each tribe was out in its array;
Each tribe save one was in its place ;—
Where were the Abencerrages ?
Of that great house remained but one ;—
The stately Musa rode alone !

He rode alone, he rode to die,
As proudly as to victory.
He knew the sable seal of fate,
On him and all his race was set ;
That night would close in blood and tears
The story of a thousand years.
His place was on the king's right hand :
  His place no more ! all stern and high,
Whatever fate befell the land,
  He rode alone, and rode to die.
The deed of blood ! The vengeance fleet !
  The double vengeance looming nigh !

Not even the Sultan dared to meet
   The glance of that majestic eye.
As far from hope, as far from fear,
   But faithful he to every tie.
His heart was calm, his fate was clear—
   He rode alone, and rode to die.

From Abdallah's forsaken hall,
To Mahmoud's mosque without the wall,
All day beneath the still white light,
In many a singly-centred fight,
The dusty battle raged and roared ;
And pennoned spear and flashing sword,
And arm of steel and casque of gold,
And horse and foot and banners rolled,
And surged tumultuously; and where
   The Moorish squadron fainter grew,
The white-plumed chieftain's sword was there,
   Their courage to renew.

He was their trust, their hope, their stay—
His voice their war-trump all the day.
Wherever hardest pressed the foe,
On Musa's buckler fell the blow ;
Wherever name of famous knight
Was shouted in the hottest fight,

'Twas Musa that the challenge met—
The faithful chief and desolate.
Where once lay orchards, woods, and farms,
  The foe spread o'er the long brown plain;
For all the West had rushed to arms,
  To drive the Moors from Spain.
And loud and fierce the cry arose,
  As closed the long lines face to face—
In wrath from friends, in scorn from foes—
  Where ride the Abencerrages?
Enveloped in the iron fold
  Of steel-clad men, the struggling Right
Was overborne, and backward rolled
  By numbers and by weight.
They long withstood them, men and horse,
  The front of spears, the plunge and press,
Till rang through all the Christian force—
  Where ride the Abencerrages?

A wave upon a serried rock,
The Moors upon the Christians broke;
A flooded river o'er its banks,
The Christians flood the Moorish ranks.
That sudden cry unmanned their host;
It told them that the day was lost;

From left to right, from front to rear,
It rose in anger and in fear,
   The vengeance of the injured race ;
It thundered in the Sultan's ear ;—
   Where ride the Abencerrages ?
Through crowded gate and narrow street
   Came cries, and oaths, and words of blame ;
Through clank of arms and tramp of feet
   Came words that closed the years of fame.
Within the wall, where all was woe—
   Without the wall, where all was lost—
Came mingled curses, loud and low,
   The anguish of a vanquished host.
But far away, behind them all,
   One little band, and resolute,
Withstood the victors like a wall,
   To guard the flight of horse and foot.
The snow-white plume the heroes led,
   The plume that led the war so well ;
The little legion surged and swayed,
   The white plume rose and fell.
It fell and rose, and rose and fell,
   And still the foes were held at bay ;
It fell, and rose not ! When it fell,
   The hero band gave way.

And plunging o'er the trampled sod,
  They muttered sideways face to face,
Oh ! had behind great Musa rode
  The warlike Abencerrages !

They rode unarmed, they rode alone,
They stood like men all turned to stone ;
They were as helpless as the dead ;
No brother's blood their hands had shed ;
Enough and more to them to know
Their flight had wrought their Tyrants' woe ;
Whate'er the ruin over all,
Their sheathèd sword had wrought his fall.
And woful was their entrance then,
  When entered they their conquered town,
A band of broken-hearted men,
  Reft of a thousand years' renown.
They rode unarmed, they rode alone ;
  They bore the Spanish troopers' scorn
With haughty heads bent sadly down,
  Like men who have so much to mourn
That any creature's praise or blame,
  Or hope or fear, or change of lot,
Is but a passing breath to them—
  They feel it, and they know it not.

But Musa, noblest of them all,
  Was followed by a nation's tears;
A ring of Christian knights his pall
  Bore on their gleaming spears.
His buckler hacked, his helmet cleft,
  His mail cut into many a shred;
The well-known plume alone was left,
  And it was dashed with red.
Through many a long and narrow street,
  And through the market-place, they bore
The peerless chief, with honours meet
  To grace the mightiest conqueror.
They bore him from the city wall,
  They bore him through the mournful town,
And in the Alhambra's banquet-hall
  They laid the hero down.

Well may the Moorish matrons weep,
The maidens' grief be loud and deep;
The strong men grieve too much for words,
The youths throw down their useless swords.
Well may the Sultan see too late
That folly is the sword of fate;
His sun had closed a day ill spent,
And starless was the firmament.

He saw his exiled people's woe,
　　He saw their galleys crowd the sea :
Not thus eight hundred years ago
　　Their fathers came from Barbary.
And fairer grew the whole bright land ;
　　And fairer still to look upon,
The stately cities, where they stand
　　All gleaming in the sun ;—
All fairer now they seemed to be,
　　The homes they ne'er shall see again ;
And where in burning Barbary
　　Are homes like those of Spain ?

III.

NOW AND THEN.

" My timorous muse
Unambitious tracks pursues ;
Does with weak, unballast wings,
About the mossy banks and springs.
About the trees' new-blossomed heads,
About the garden's painted beds,
About the fields and flowery meads,
And all inferior beauteous things ;
Like the laborious bee,
For little drops of honey flee,
And then with humble sweets contents her industrie."
—COWLEY'S *Ode in Praise of Pindar*,
imitated from Horace.

THE BANNERS OF OLD.

FAR down the long vista of shadowy ages
   Ye see the fierce tumult of battle alone;
No light on the war-cloud the day-dawn presages,
   With faith to the temple or law to the throne.
The desolate earth hid in splendours volcanic,
   In earth-born glory what symbol is there?
What hope that can lift it o'er life scarce organic,
   Late blossoming out of a silent despair?

What purpose of man, or what life-theme of nations,
   From out this red struggle for mastery springs?
What growth from this death-wreck of war's desola-
      tions?
What hope where the sword is the plaything of kings,
Who make, in their passion, man's lordliest token
   The weapon of envy, oppression, and pride?
See, down through the ages the red sword lies broken,
   While justice alone keeps it clear by its side!

The banners of old through the war-clouds are breaking,
　　Like golden-winged eagles half hid in the mist;
The earth with the tread of her armies is shaking,
　　And knows but in song of the sweetness of rest.
I doubt not some purpose, all richly resultant,
　　Runs through this rude chaos of turmoil and strife;
But where shall we greet, with a spirit exultant,
　　Some Banner to lead the brave battle of life?

There hangeth full many a war-worn standard,
　　All dusty, in many a high olden hall;
And brave hearts by thousands their best blood have
　　　squandered,
　　Of old, 'neath the folds that so peacefully fall.
We see where they wave o'er the land's highest chivalry,
　　Where many a famous old warrior lies;
Or gaily unrolled at the tournament's rivalry,
　　Shine in the light of earth's loveliest eyes;

And fair maidens, may be, have wove their devices,
　　And sung o'er their looms of the warrior time;
And still o'er the picture the fancy rejoices,
　　Nor deems them the emblems of rapine and crime.
For well do we love them, all faded and tattered,
　　Though blood may have blackened both crimson
　　　and gold;

Though waving all night in the sighs of the slaughtered,
   We love them, the war-worn Banners of Old.

But are they the standards for freemen to follow,
   That warred with the freedom and manhood of man,
That set up their symbols as blood-stained and hollow
   As any rude idol in all Hindustan?
Then where is the banner far floating in glory,
   The hope of our manhood, the dream of our youth?
In the light of to-day or the halo of story,
   Where seek we the Banner of Freedom and Truth?

How fondly we gaze on the grand old Greek heroes:
   The glories of many an ancient Greek town;
The conquering Romans, whose triumphs ensnare us
   To love for the strong-handed victor's renown!
We follow the course of earth's proudest invaders,
   Half dead to the woe, to the desert half blind,
And linger with love round the gallant Crusaders,
   Nor bear the great Preacher of peace in our mind.

We see the fierce might and the bold-hearted daring
   That cleave like a sword their red way to the crown;
The woe shrieking far o'er their pathway unsparing;
   The song like the music of battle rings down.

We see them and long for that glorious banner
 That Faith looketh for, and that Hope hath fore-
  told—
The Banner of Justice, of Freedom, and Honour,
 More glorious far than the Banners of Old.

Our own noble flag, how we love and revere it!
 May beauty shine round it for ever and aye!
And blest in their might be the brave hands that
  ˋbear it,
 Their pathway of splendour as bright as the day.
But all its rare grandeur, its mighty old story,
 Are only the founts of a kinglier time,
Where floats in the light of its shadowless glory,
 The banner that leads the whole earth to its prime.

The Scottish heart follows its Bruce and its Wallace,
 As follows the Switzer's its brave William Tell;
And long be their story remembered, to tell us
 The time-hallowed spots where they battled so well.
Where'er there be standards of heath and of altar—
 The flags that a land's kneeling mothers have
  blessed—
The brave hearts beneath them, we know, will not
  falter
 To strike for the free, or to free the oppressed.

All honour be round them while men's eyes grow
    clearer
To every old purpose that lives in renown ;
We'll hold their old triumphs all dear, and still dearer
    The place where the light of their glory went down;
And so, with the banners of fame in the vanward,
    Abroad o'er the tombs of our fathers unrolled :
But surely, though slowly, comes one floating onward,
    More glorious far than the Banners of Old.

And bright-fingered angels its legends have painted,
    With hues from the rainbow and gold from the sun;
And Truth, Love, and Peace on its folds are indented,
    To gather the far-scattered nations in one.
Abroad on the breast of winds we'll unfold it,
    To win back to earth the bright hopes of her youth,
The fruits of her promise,—while all who behold it
    Shall greet the fair Banner of Freedom and Truth.

THE SILVER CITY.

My Silver City by the Sea,
   Thy white foot rests on golden sands;
A radiant robe encircles thee
   Of woody hills and garden lands.
I'll lift my cap and sing thy praise,
   By silent Don and crystal Dee;
Oh, bravely gentle all thy days,
   Fair City by the Sea!
Bonaillie, O Bonaillie!
   My Silver City by the Sea.

I'll love thee till my tongue be mute,
   For all thy fame of ancient years,
Thy tender heart and resolute,
   Thy tale of glory and of tears;
The might that from thy bosom springs,
   To fire thy sons where'er they be,

And for a thousand noble things—
  Brave City by the Sea !
Bonaillie, O Bonaillie !
  My Silver City by the Sea.

Fair City of the Rivers Twain,
  No child of idle dalliance thou ;
The silvery borders of thy train
  Come from the rugged mountains' brow.
And well I wot thy best of wealth,
  The wind of God brings fairly free,
Thy brave bright eyes and ruddy health,
  Fair City by the Sea !
Bonaillie, O Bonaillie ! *
  My Silver City by the Sea.

* Bonaillie, an old Scottish toast, from the French *Bon allez.*

WELCOME!

SHE'S the flower of the race of the fair-haired kings,
   And her brow is as white as the foam :
And we'll welcome her till the welkin rings,
   As the light of our young Lord's home.
Like the Queen of our love—and, the world can tell,
   . Of our darling and our pride—
Like the Queen of our love we will guard her well,
   As she stands by her young Lord's side :
      And the waves roll out their Welcome,
        As they break on the yellow sand ;
      And the people shout their Welcome—
      And their mighty-voiced Welcome
        Is an anthem in the land :
For who but the Sea-King's child should be
The Bride of the Sea-King's land ?

From the silver ring where her sisters are,
  From their arms of holy white,
She comes, from the East, like a splendid star,
  With its golden locks of light.
Like the joy of our homes, when our hearts were stirred
  By the first-love breath of spring,
We will welcome her as our halcyon bird,
  With the summer on its wing.
      And the joy-bells fling their Welcome
        From the minsters old and grand;
      And the hamlets ring their Welcome—
      Their simple-hearted Welcome—
        To the Bride of the Brave Old Land:
    For who but the Sea-King's child should be
    The Bride of the Sea-King's land?

'Twas the mightiest Lord of the days of yore,
  And he wept salt tears to see
How the Viking's galleys swept his shore,
  With the Danebrog waving free.
And our fathers met them, blade to blade,
  In the wars of a hundred years;
But the soft blue eyes of our Danish maid—
  They are more than the Danish spears.
      And the cannons thunder Welcome
        All along the battled strand;

And the trumpets sound their Welcome—
Their wild and warlike Welcome—
   To the Bride of the Brave Old Land:
For who but the Sea-King's child should be
The Bride of the Sea-King's land?

She comes in the light of her loveliness—
   In the joy of her golden days;
And the hands of the people are raised to bless,
   And their voice in songs of praise:
And the thunder-peals of welcome swell
   Through the cities' crimson air;
And the joy of the hamlets is heard as well,
   Though 'tis simple as their prayer;
      And the mighty voice of Welcome,
         Of true heart and trusty hand—
      The Realm's rejoicing Welcome—
      Fills the heaven's blue vault with Welcome,
         Like an anthem of the land:
For who but the Sea-King's child should be
The Bride of the Sea-King's land?

And the Queen of our hearts is the Queen of the Sea;
   And as long as the sea rolls on,
May the love of the faithful, the faith of the free,
   Be around her children's throne.

And whate'er be the storms that the waters toss,
   May their banner, in peace and war,
Be the sceptre that waves to the Southern Cross,
   And that shines to the Northern Star.
      And the thunder-burst of Welcome,
        Like a storm-surge on the strand,
      Is the wonder-burst of Welcome—
      Of the far-resounding Welcome—
      Of a whole rejoicing land :
For who but the Sea-King's child should be
The Bride of the Brave Old Land !

March 3, 1863.

THE PIOBRACH O' KINREEN.

Och, hey! Kinreen o' the Dee,
Kinreen o' the Dee,
Kinreen o' the Dee—
Och, hey! Kinreen o' the Dee.
I'll blaw up my chanter
I've sounded fu' weel,
To mony a ranter
In mony a reel;
An' pour a' my heart i' the win'bag wi' glee:
Och, hey! Kinreen o' the Dee.
For licht was the lauchter on bonny Kinreen,
An' licht was the fitt-fa' that danced o'er the green,
An' licht were the hearts a', and lichtsome the eyne.
Och, hey! Kinreen o' the Dee, &c.

The auld hoose is bare noo,
　　A cauld hoose to me ;
The hearth is nae mair noo
　　The centre o' glee ;
Nae mair for the bairnies the bield it has been :
　　Och, hey ! for bonny Kinreen.
The auld folk, the young folk, the wee anes an' a',
A hunder years' hame birds are harried awa—
Are harried an' hameless whatever winds blaw.
　　Och, hey ! Kinreen o' the Dee, &c.

Fareweel my auld plew-lan' !
　　I'll never mair plew it ;
Fareweel my auld plew, an'
　　The auld yaud that drew it !
Fareweel my auld kail-yard, ilk bush an' ilk tree !
　　Och, hey ! Kinreen o' the Dee ;
Fareweel the auld braes that my han' keepit green ;
Fareweel the auld ways where we wandered unseen,
Ere the licht o' my hearth cam to bonny Kinreen.
　　Och, hey ! Kinreen o' the Dee, &c.

The auld kirk looks up o'er
The dreesome auld dead,
Like a saint speaking hope o'er
Some sorrowfu' bed.
Fareweel the auld kirk, and fareweel the kirk-green !
They speak o' a far better hame than Kinreen ;
The place we wa'd cling to, puir simple auld fules,
O' oor births an' oor bridals, oor blisses an' dools,
Where the wee bits o' bairnies lie cauld i' the mools.
Och, hey ! Kinreen o' the Dee, &c.

I afttimes ha'e wondered
If deer be as dear,
As sweet ties o' kindred
To peasant or peer ;
As the tie to the hames o' the lan'-born be :
Och, hey ! Kinreen o' the Dee.
The heather that blossoms unkent on the moor,
Wad dee in the bonniest greenhouse, I'm sure,
To the wonder o' mony a forran-lan' flower.
Och, hey ! Kinreen o' the Dee, &c.

Though little the thing be
Oor ain we can ca',
That little we cling be
The mair that it's sma'.

Though puir was oor hame, and though wild was the
scene,
'Twas the hame o' oor hearts, it was bonny Kinreen ;
And noo we maun leave it, baith grey head and bairn;
Maun leave it to fatten the deer o' Knock Cairn,
An' a' frae Lochlee to o' Morven o' Gairn.

Och, hey ! Kinreen o' the Dee,
Kinreen o' the Dee,
Kinreen o' the Dee—
Sae fareweel for ever, Kinreen o' the Dee !

LOVE AND JOY.

Rosy Joy and blushing Love, once hand in hand you
    roamed together,
Slackly hung your flowery chains, whose blossoms
    ne'er seemed doomed to wither ;
Smiles that mocked the summer dawn, with all the
    light of beauty crowned you :
Rosy Joy and blushing Love, where have ye left the
    wreaths that bound you ?

Where's the hope that knew no fear, and where's the
    love-light never fading ?
Where's the eye that knew no tear, save that of bliss-
    ful rapture's shading ?
Where's the ceaseless summer tide, that cheered their
    fairy paths who found you ?
Rosy Joy and blushing Love, where. are the flowery
    chains that bound you ?

Blushing cheeks, and melting eyes that gazed upon
  each other ever;
Hearts that beat with happy sighs, all dreaming still
  of parting never;
Songs as sweet as angels' lyres, made pleasant every
  spot around you :
Rosy Joy and blushing Love, oh, where's the flowery
  wreath that bound you?

Love sits and weeps, for she is true, while Joy in courtly
  halls is dancing;
Joy is decked with gems anew, while Love's soft eyes
  with tears are glancing—
Tears more bright than all the gems with which e'er
  kingly hands have crowned you :
Rosy Joy and blushing Love, oh, where's the flowery
  wreath that bound you?

Twine again your flowery chain, for why should twain
  so meet be parted?
Joy is heartless without Love, and joyless Love is
  broken-hearted;
Twine again your flowery chain, that Heaven's own
  hand first threw around you :
Rosy Joy and blushing Love, bring back the flowery
  links that bound you.

TO THE SCOTTISH LYRE.

A PINDARIC ODE.

THE sweet-stringed Scottish lyre !
The harp of that old minstrel land,
That never lacked a master's hand,
Or martyr's faith, or patriot's fire,
    The singer to inspire ;
Or soft emotion pearling all the eyes
Of listening ages with responsive tears,
To clothe with love the memorable years,
To give the suns new promise as they rise :
Ring out for ever to the white-robed band
Who sit among the old melodious dead,
Each in the light which he himself has shed,
    With resonant command,
    Lighting up the old renowns,
    Lighting up the laurel crowns,
    Pouring forth the songs of praise
    Through the old heroic days,

In the wisest words of sages,
On the deeds of all the ages,
In deep harmonious music through the land.

And sweetly ever to the loved of all,
The household friend, the bard of great and small,
Who showed a loving nature face to face,
Its inmost spirit glorified in song,
And passed away to fill his kingly place
Among the white-robed throng
That walk behind the prophets.   Evermore
Ring out the joyous strain as heretofore,
Love on the hand and rapture on the wire,
To join with wider joy the wider choir,
Where immemorial sea of song resounds
Its ancient anthems like the deep that bounds
The golden circle of our sacred shore.

The Muses heard him singing at the plough,
And on his head their inspiration poured.
Thus when Apollo doubly bent his bow,
And made a harp-string of the ringing cord,
The souls of men a new-born pleasure found
        In that sweet sound
That rang through all green Thessaly of old,
Till from the hunter's bow the lyre of gold,

Made perfect by the god,
Poured light and tenderness through ancient lays
　　Till even the Olympian abode
　　Resounded to its praise.

　　And when the muse her mantle threw
　　　Around the lowly peasant boy,
　　She bade him sweep the lyre anew
　　　O'er all its ancient chords of joy;
　　Shrive his brethren's inmost spirit,
　　　Wake them to their fathers' glory;
　　Teach their children how to wear it,
　　　Widening still the noble story;—
Words of light on golden pages
Sounding through the choral ages;
And the grand old harp is pealing,
Ever pealing far and near.
Where's the ear that doth not hear?
Where's the heart it doth not cheer?
That old melodious lyre unsealing
All the heart's bright fountains deep and dear.

Honour to those who spend contented days
　　In making fair the paths of other men,
In digging wells and planting shady ways,
　　Where weary feet may rest and rise again.

And what although his path was hard—
And what although his joy was marred
    By poverty and wrong?
Above his fortunes and his foes,
The lonely peasant youth arose
    A paladin of song;
And with him rose the peasant race,
And looked the proudest face to face.
He brought new sunshine to their fields,
New pleasure to their humblest bields,
New hope to light their lonely ways,
New light to cheer them all their days.
And beauty grew beneath his hand
More beautiful.   With sweet surprise
Men gazing through his ardent eyes
Saw new-born glory in the land.
His very laughter, loud and free,
The music of his manly mirth,
Is ringing over all the earth,
And to the farthest island of the sea.

      And his sadness
      Was a gladness,
   And the passion of his tears
      Left a pleasure,
      Left a treasure,

Left a blessing to the years ;
Touched our hearts with deep emotion,
Glowing with their purple tide,
While his own was breaking slowly—
His so loved, so lost, so lowly,
Doomed to drink life's saddest potion ;
And we grieve not that he died,
But that he died neglected wholly,
He who is a nation's pride.

Crown the wine-cup, wreathe the lyre, ·
Fill the measure of his fame ;
See from eyes with triumph beaming
Sweet atoning tears are streaming,
While from far across the ocean
Comes a shout of deep devotion,
Swelling louder, rising higher,
At the utterance of his name,
To overflow with love our former shame.

Alas ! the time when pride and passions met,
In his green wilderness of noble years ;
Though love looks on more loving for regret,
And like a mother smiles away her tears.

But whether saints or sages,
Who are they who blame the ages,
That they pass not through their story
Ever garmented with light?
Let such the minstrel scorn,
Whose head is clothed with glory,
Like an Alp against the morn,
Because his feet are hidden in the night.

True, as from other times he bore
Their beauty, he some darker traces
Of their rude old fashions wore;
And swept along in all men's faces,
With a noble ardour glowing,
With a fearless vehemence showing
Every passionate thought that swayed him,
Just the man that Nature made him,—
Rough and real, kind and free,
Brave and true as man could be;
Brown with days of honest toil—
Loosely robed in manly graces—
Bearing something of the soil
With him to the highest places.
Pulsing through a thousand years,
The land's old life-blood filled his veins;

M

Pulsing through a thousand years,
The land's old spirit fired his strains ;
These were not perfection wholly :
When we censure such as he,
Mind our fathers' casual folly,
Mind their ancient Bacchic glee. ·

Yet thou, O Lyre ! hast seen repentant tears
Roll hot and heavy o'er his sunken cheek,
And heard the sigh that rose through faded years,
With memories that the tongue forbore to speak.
And thou hast seen his heart by passion torn
Unveil itself before the Father's face,
And that proud lip of thunder and of scorn
Grow tremulous with childlike tenderness ;
And healing sorrow watch him all the night,
And love subdue the ardour of his eyes,
And passion fade before the blessèd light
That came to guide the minstrel to the skies.

So let the shadow sleep beside the clay,
And that great front that rises through the past,
        No longer overcast,
Rest on the light of love's immortal ray.
Through all our hearts from prince to peasant boy,
Ring out for ever to the glorious dead,
Who round our hills such sweet effulgence shed,

And touched the ages as they pass with joy;
Who through our souls new streams of rapture poured,
Whose tones of sweetness to the world belong;
Whose mirth still radiates round our festive board,
While household joys are sweeter for his song;
Who o'er the earth has poured his wondrous strain,
As these vast rivers of the torrid west
Roll widely warm their waters through the main,
To make the soil of distant lands more blest.
And we, in grasping England's royal hand,
Remember still the minstrels of the land,
All robed and glorified in their renown,
Each with his lyre and his immortal crown,
And pouring round us one triumphant flood
Of song that pulses through our hearts like blood—
That fired our fathers in the days of old
With greater love for freedom than for gold,
And made its home, their mountain dwelling-place,
The royal cradle of a fearless race;
And while that love goes round the sacred shore,
With all the fervent passion felt of yore,
Through all the greatness of the common name,
Shall glow the lustre of our Minstrel's fame.

NOTE.—The above Ode was one of the poems "highly com-
mended" by the Judges at the Crystal Palace Competition on
the Centenary of Burns' Birthday 1859.

THE AULD MAN'S WELCOME.

THE spring is sweet wi' a' its birds,
　An' sweet the summer's shady ways,
But kindly smiles an' gentle words
　Are sweeter in oor winter days.
And noo it's my December time—
　Nay, dawtie, dry yer winsome e'e—
My head is white wi' frosty rime,
　An' bide or gang, I'll welcome be.
Among the loved, among the Leal,
　There's many a friend to welcome me.

Sweet were the eyne that gazed in mine,
　An' summer shone through a' the year;
They've lichted many a dream sin' syne,
　An' died in many a wauknin' tear.
I see them as in life's day-daw,
　As fair as heaven's ain blue to me;

Ye'll greet the less when I'm awa,
   That Her dear eyne will welcome me ;
Will welcome me among the Leal—
   That Her dear eyne will welcome me.

The burnie sings the same auld tune
   It sang when first for me it flowed ;
An' yon grey hawthorn's flowers in June
   Are dearer far than draps o' gowd ;
For there I hear Her whispers sweet,
   Her breath hangs roon' the trystin' tree ;
An' aft I think when we shall meet,
   The well-kenned voice will welcome me ;
Will welcome me among the Leal—
   The sweet, sweet lips will welcome me !

The friends wha cheered oor hamely hearth,
   Their voices a' are silent noo—
The merry men wi' a' their mirth,
   The blithe, the manly, and the true.
The time passed by wi' kindly cheer,
   Like some auld lilt o' household glee ;
Their well-kenned voices aft I hear,
   And think that they will welcome me ;
Will welcome me among the Leal—
   And think that they will welcome me.

At kirk an' market many a face
 Wad wi' its ae-fauld welcome shine ;
Wi' many a grasp o' friendliness
 Some frank auld hand took hauld o' mine.
An' though the young be mair than kind—
 And kinder folk there couldna be—
The auld are maist to my auld mind !
 They'll come wi' Her to welcome me ;
To welcome me among the Leal—
 They'll come wi' Her to welcome me.

The stars are risin' ane by ane,
 To let the bits o' blossoms sleep ;
We're never in this world alane,
 There's aye a watch for some to keep.
But up an' doon, o'er ane an a',
 Ane keeps His watch o'er lan' an' sea—
The Hand that tents the sparrow's fa'
 I think will maybe welcome me ;
Will welcome me among the Leal—
 I think will maybe welcome me.

It's nae that auld hearth-love is less,
 Or auld hame pleasures faint or few ;
It's nae for lack o' kindliness—
 I'll aye ha'e that while I ha'e you :

But dear to me is that auld past;
   Whate'er the present bliss may be :
An' never grudge the thochts I cast
   On those wha sune will welcome me ;
Will welcome me among the Leal—
   On those wha sune will welcome me.

THE BORDER MAN.

A NORTHUMBRIAN SONG.

CHANGED days noo, hinny,
　　Sair awa' noo;
Changed days noo, hinny,
　　A' but love o' thoo.

When first I took thy maiden han',
　　And sou'ht thy love for mine,
There wis nae baulder border man
　　In a' the Ward o' Tyne.
Mair buirdly aye I grew each day,
　　Mair bauld wi' love I grew,
Though rough o' han' for ready fray,
　　My heart could hallow thoo.
　　　　Sair changed noo, hinny,
　　　　　Sair changed noo;
　　　　Sair changed noo, hinny,
　　　　　Sin' I kenned thoo.

Thee wis a bonny apple-tree,
  Wi' a' thy flowers in May;
An' I thy gardener lad wad be,
  To keep thoo trim an' gay.
Thee's ruddy sweet wi' apples yet,
  It's a' my hert to pu',
Though I can barely lift a fitt
  To delve my garden noo.
      Bright days then, hinny,
        Changed times noo.;
      Sair awa' noo, hinny,
        Sin' I kenned thoo.

A man to daunt me, man to man,
  O'er a' the Marches three;
A horse to balk my bridle-han'
  I wad gane far to see;
But thee so fair, my love so rare,
  My rose, my snow-white doo!
Wad led me wi' ae silken hair,
  The wide, wide worrold thro'.
      Changed days noo, hinny,
        Sair awa' noo;
      Changed days noo, hinny,
        A' but love o' thoo.

That wonnot change, that cannot change,
   That's grown from year to year,
Abune the Sun it wad be strange
   To love thee less than here :
For aye I smooth thy silken hair,
   An' kiss thy rosy mou ;
There's no change to me there,
   There's no change in thoo.
     Change be a' here, hinny,
      Changed days noo ;
    Sair awa' noo, hinny,
      Sin' I kenned thoo.

WHY DO THEY DIE?

In the fresh glow of beauty, the first flush of light,
Should the day-dawn be quenched in the shadow of
     night,
And the star of the morning pass fruitless away,
And break to the earth its bright promise of day?
Ah, no! Then why fade thus earth's loveliest flowers?
  And why do the young and the beautiful die,
Ere they drink the first rapture of summer's bright
     hours,
  Ere the brow hath a cloud or the bosom a sigh?

They spring like young fountains, as pure and as free,
To freshen the earth where their pathways may be;
They brighten the cot and they gladden the hall,
In every land blooming, the loved ones of all:

But, alas! there are gems on the night-clouded earth
   Only lit by the far-away stars of the sky;
The gathering cloud darkens their light at its birth,
   And like these do the young and the beautiful die.

With love ever gazing through summer-lit eyes,
The free falcon glance where no faithlessness lies,
The glad tones of laughter, the song and the smile,
And the low gentle voice that each care can beguile;
They come in the beauty of shadowless truth,
   Bringing flowers to the green tree and leaves to the
      bare;
They wreathe their fair brows with the bright dreams
      of youth,
   Like the garlanded dreamers as fleeting as fair.

Oh, could not earth nurture such flowers where they
      grew,
With its love like the sunshine, its tears like the dew?
And could not hope foster, nor happiness bind,
Nor the shadow of sorrow, dark brooding behind,
Detain them, the loved ones?   Ah, no! day by day
   We list for some footfall in vain at the door;
Their sweet songs of joy from the hearth pass away,
   And the woodlands re-echo their laughter no more.

Be hushed! they are happy who die in their youth,
Untainted their heart and unsullied their truth;
Unbent by the burden of earth's many ills,
Where misery saddens and heartlessness chills.
Though like youth's own bright visions they come and
     depart,
  And leave not a trace to the lovingest eye,
In the hope and the love and the trust of the heart,
  They live ever beautiful—never can die.

THE ROSE-A-LYNDSAYE.

THERE are seven fair flowers in yon green wood,
   On a bush in the woods o' Lyndsaye;
There are sax braw flowers an' ae bonny bud,
   Oh! the bonniest flower in Lyndsaye.
An' weel I luve the bonny rathe rose—
   The bonny, bonny Rose-a-Lyndsaye;
An' I'll big my bower o' the forest-boughs,
   An' I'll dee in the green woods o' Lyndsaye.

There be jewels upon her snaw-white breast,
   An' her hair is wreathed wi' garlan's—
A cord o' gowd is round her waist,
   An' her shoon are sewed wi' pearlins:
An' oh! she is the bonny, bonny rose—
   She's the gentle Rose-a-Lyndsaye;
An' I'll big my bower where my blossom blows,
   An' I'll dee in the green woods o' Lyndsaye.

Her face 'tis like the evenin' lake
　　That the birk and the willow fringes ;
Whase peace the wild winds canna' break,
　　Or but its beauty changes.
And she is aye my bonny, bonny rose—
　　She's the bonny young Rose-a-Lyndsaye ;
An' ae blink o' her e'e wad be dearer to me
　　Than the wale o' the lands o' Lyndsaye.

Her voice is like the gentle lute
　　When minstrels tales are tellin' :
An' ever saftly falls her fute,
　　Like autumn leaves a fallin'.
An' oh ! she's the rose, she's the bonny, bonny rose—
　　She's the snaw-white Rose-a-Lyndsaye ;
An' I'll kiss her steps at the gloamin' close,
　　Through the flowerie woods o' Lyndsaye.

It's sax brave sons has the good Lord James,
　　Their worth I downa' gainsay;
For Scotsmen ken they are gallant men,
　　The children o' the Lyndsaye :
An' proud are they o' their bonny rathe rose,
　　O' the fair young Rose-a-Lyndsaye ;
But pride for luve makes friends like foes,
　　An' grief in the green woods o' Lyndsaye.

But shall I weep. where I daurna' woo,
  An' the land in sic disorder?
My arm is strong, my heart is true,
  And the Percie's over the border:
Then fare ye weel, my bonny, bonny rose,
  And blest be the woods o' Lyndsaye;
I'll gild my spurs i'. the bluid o' her foes,
  An' come back to the Rose-a-Lyndsaye.

An intimate friend of Forsyth's (Dr Walter C. Smith) whose wide knowledge of the subject was ample warrant for his assertion, in Forsyth's house one night that he could at once detect a genuine ancient ballad from the best modern imitation that ever was made, was deceived with the foregoing. Forsyth handed him "The Rose-a-Lyndsaye," asking him his opinion as to its antiquity. Dr S. read it and immediately pronounced it a genuine old ballad & a perfect gem. He asked Forsyth where he had fallen in with it, but was evasively answered and it was some time after before he learned that he had been cheated with one of Forsyth's own compositions.

                                    J.D.W.

THE FEAST OF TABERNACLES.

"Ye shall dwell in booths seven days; all that are Israelites born shall dwell in booths: that your generations may know that I made the children of Israel to dwell in booths, when I brought them out of the land of Egypt."—Levit. xxiii. 42, 43.

GIVE me the boughs, my children—
 The boughs of the richest leaves;
While wand o'er wand your mother's hand
 Around the pillar weaves.

Give the flowers to her, my children,
 Whose love has been flower and leaf
To me, like the spring-time to the tree
 To chase the winter's grief.

It was joyous in Judah's vineyards,
 When o'er the country wide
They sat within their myrtle-groves,
 The households side by side.

N

It was joyous in Judah's vineyards
  When our graceful maids went forth,
With music and with dancing,
  To make glad the bounteous earth.

It was joyous in Judah's vineyards
  When the bursting grape they crushed;
But the heathen rage in our heritage,
  And the voice of joy is hushed.

There's a home to the Eastern pagan,
  Though he kneel to stock and stone;
Each Christian race has its dwelling-place,
  But the people of God have none.

Like our ancient pilgrim fathers
  Through the wilderness we stray;
But there is none like Amram's son
  To guide our weary way.

But the glory of olden wonders
  Is a glory ever new,
And the promises to the ancient race
  Remain for ever true.

For the day-dawn is not surer
  Than the day-dawn yet to be
On the sunny hills of Judah and
  The shores of Galilee ;

And Zion of a thousand songs
  To which our people went,
All singing in triumphant voice
  The Songs of the Ascent.

And now in humble hopefulness
  We will sing Jehovah's praise
In that bright home of times to come,
  In the land of the ancient days.

Our voices in glad hosannas
  We will raise with joy divine,
To praise the Hand that fills the land
  With corn, and oil, and wine.

Though silent be the song of joy
  On Zion's holy hill,
In Judah's clime of summer time
  The vine is purpling still.

Though they see the abomination
  Of desolation stand
In the Holy Place, and the Ancient Race
  Are strangers in the land ;

We know Jehovah reigneth,
  And beholds His people's woes ;
And there the sacred bower they build
  Of the immemorial boughs.

In the soft old Syrian sunshine
  The purple vats they fill,
Where the palm-tree droops o'er Parphar,
  Under Hermon's gladsome hill ;

Damascus has rainbow gardens
  That are blooming like the rose,
There too they build the sacred bower
  Of the immemorial boughs.

And these are but fading branches,
  But they bring from their old abode
The bliss of a lingering loveliness
  And the living breath of God.

Then bring me the boughs, my children,
　　While your mother is twining flowers,
And sing a lay of the ancient day
　　To lighten our pilgrim hours.

We will welcome the glowing vintage,
　　As our fathers did of old,
When soft Judea's sunny hills
　　Were clad in autumn's gold.

We will welcome the glowing vintage,
　　Though for us there droops no vine,
Nor the citron, nor the pomegranate
　　Of purple Palestine.

The voice of the Lord, from Sinai,
　　Still resounds above the plain ;
The cloud by day, and the midnight ray,
　　In the promises remain ;

And afar by the Jordan's waters,
　　By the Thames' triumphant tide ;
By the Tiber, and the Danube, and
　　Where'er our race abide,

The voice of their beauteous daughters
　Is heard in sacred song ;
As they sing the ancient promises
　In the sweet old Hebrew tongue.

They are singing the songs of Zion,
　And the hope of David's race,
That not the tears of captive years
　By Babel could efface.

They are singing the songs of Zion,
　And the hope that did not fall,
When the banner of the Maccabees
　Was borne from Salem's wall :

And with timbrels and with dancing
　Under many a northern sky,
They sing of climes in coming times,
　Where Canaan's beauties lie.

Then bring me the boughs, my children—
　Bring the richest in leafy bloom ;
The wilderness is our dwelling-place,
　Oh that Pisgah were our tomb !

We will sing our glad hosannas,
　For our hope is all divine,
To praise the hand that fills the land
　With corn, and oil, and wine.

.　　.　　.　　.　　.

Though a poor Whitechapel Hebrew,
　He his festal bower had made ;
And round him there three thousand years
　A dim old halo shed.

And wondering much and pondering more
　O'er what I heard and saw,
I said, When shall the deeper Love
　Rule like the formal Law ?

BROKEN.

FAREWELL, bright brand! the freeman's hand
Alone can wield a sword like thee.
    We've bravely stood
      Among the dead,
    Both red with blood,
      When we were free;
But now farewell, thou noble blade !
The captive's hand is not for thee.

No more in fields of ringing shields,
And gleaming helms, with warlike glee,
    Thy light shall flash
      Above my head,
    As in the crash
      When we were free.
So fare ye well, thou noble blade !
The captive's hand is not for thee.

Oh, never shall the foeman's thrall
In thy bright face his blushes see,
But glory o'er
Thee radiance shed
As heretofore,
When we were free.
So fare ye well, thou noble blade !
The captive's hand is not for thee.

THE ROSES.

"Gather rosebuds while you may,
Old Time is still a-flying."—HERRICK.

WE'LL go and gather roses,
　　While summer beauties last,
Ere the cloud its coming shows us,
　　By shadows round us cast.
We'll go with song and laughter,
　　Light heart and sunny eye,
And think on care hereafter,
　　'Neath winter's cauldrife sky.
We'll go and gather roses—summer's sweetest roses—
　　Through the bowers of beauty vaunted,
　　Woods where ceaseless songs are chaunted,
　　And by fountains fairy-haunted,
　　　　Go and gather roses.

We'll go and gather roses,
　　Our flowery path along;

Each step some sweet discloses,
   Each breath is full of song.
The merry waters falling,
   The wild birds as they sing,
The woodland fays are calling
   From out the fairy ring,
To go and gather roses—bonny budding roses—
   To wreath young beauty's flowing hair,
   With sisters meet to blossom there;
   Sweetest flowers, though ne'er so fair
   As earth's own peerless roses.

We'll go and gather roses
   Where'er they brightest be,
While a thousand radiant glosses
   Glint o'er the gow'ny lea !
Ere the loveliness of summer
   And its happy hours depart,
And the sunshine waxes dimmer
   On the hills and in the heart,
We'll go and gather roses—dewy-bosomed roses—
   The cloud may come before we wot,
   The tear before we dream o't;
   Then make the best of every lot,
   And gather summer roses.

ABOVE THE SNOW.

A SONG.

TELL me not of loveliness fading,
  Dream not, dearest, of love's decay;
Like the roses blooming and shedding
  All their bliss on a summer day.

No, love, no; adown by the valleys
  Flowers are thoughts, and they come and go;
But the summer is with us always,
  While our hearts are above the snow.

Gentle Time will never bereave thee
  Of a beauty that love hath blest;
He will gifts of memory leave thee,
  That will make him a welcome guest.

Pictures Time will make half sainted,
   If the colours be made to stand;
Such as grand old masters have painted,
   That with years grow still more grand.

Age will come, but we will remember
   All the brightness of life's young day;
O'er the face of frosty December,
   Scatter bloom from its glowing May.

Bloom from out thy bountiful hand, love,
   Foliage fairer than robes of spring;
Smiles that light to beauty the land, love,
   Songs more sweet than bird could sing.

Thou art fair, and I ever merry,
   Loving, laughing the livelong day;
Dream not, then, of love growing weary,
   Dream not beauty can die away.

No, love, no; adown by the valleys
   Flowers are thoughts, and they come and go;
But the summer it lasteth always,
   While our hearts are above the snow.

LADY LOO.

To ride in state with grandeur,
Or walk afoot with love,
You have this day, my darling may, your choice
between the two :
By sunny streams to wander,
Through stately halls to move,
To be the lady of the land, or my own pretty Loo—
Loo, Loo, pretty Loo !

This lord's good name I value
As truly as mine own ;
Whiche'er ye wed, my darling maid, ye will not wed
to rue :
'Tis true, if he but tell you
He'll love but you alone ;
But ne'er will he love lady as I love pretty Loo—
Loo, Loo, pretty Loo !

I've never dreamt of grandeur,
   This lord I've never seen,
But well you know already, I'll walk afoot with you.
   Then through life's ways we'll wander,
   My love, my life, my queen,
To all, the land's sweet lady, to me my pretty Loo—
   Loo, Loo, Lady Loo!

THE LOVERS' SEAT.

An' is't awa', that auld stane seat,
   That eased the Stocket brae,
Where lads and lasses used to meet,
   Through a' the gloamin' grey?
There's mony a hearth that's blithe and bien,
   Sprung up frae whispers sweet
That lovin' lips hae breathed at e'en
   Roun' that auld lovers' seat—
      Auld Lovers' Seat.

It's five-and-fifty years and mair
   Sin' I brocht hame a bride;
I wooed her whan a lassie there,
   To sit at my fireside;
An' is it gane, wi' a' the days
   Whan we were won't to meet;
An' is it gane, wi' a the lays
   We sang on that auld seat—
      Auld Lovers' Seat?

Through summer sun and winter's win'
   It aye had shiel' and shade,
An' hield, whan drift wis blawin' blin',
   Twa lovers in ae plaid.
The cauldest nicht o' frost an' snaw,
   It keepit aye its heat;
I never passed it but I saw
   'Twas aye the Lovers' Seat—
      Auld Lovers' Seat.

Their faces, a' the simmer, they
   Had aye a happy smirk;
Their een, when nichts grew dimmer, they
   Made moonlicht i' the mirk.
The road that wad been eerie, where
   The ancient tree-taps meet,
Sweet whispers aye made cheerie there
   Roun' that auld Lovers' Seat—
      Auld Lovers' Seat.

THE RINGS.

"It was my torquoise;
I had it of Leah when I was a bachelor."
—*Merchant of Venice.*

How sadly beautiful the long last sleep
And brow unwrinkled of the early taken,
The white cheek wet with tears of those who weep
And pray that the sweet sleeper may awaken !
There Peace and Beauty are as one.   They lie
Like some hushed joy beyond the reach of change,
Left there to let our last hopes gently die,
And slowly, through this sudden grief and strange.

The last faint ray of sunset lights the skies,
But not for her.   The vacant east will shine
With dawns of joy : but not for us will rise
The cloudy curtains of these orbs divine,
These founts of living bliss again disclose,
And the auroral blush of morning light.
Ah ! who shall clothe with bloom the faded rose,
Or ask of heaven to stay an angel's flight ?

There lie her roses.   None of them are withered—
She plucked them for a wreath to wear to-day;
Still fresh and fair! although the bloom be gath-
    ered
From her fair cheek more beautiful than they.
More beautiful!   This morn we saw her glide
So angel-like by bush and leafy bowers;
She seemed the spirit of the summer-tide
Surprised at her sweet task of making flowers.

And grieve not that it was a festive moment,
When like a bright light quenched, her spirit fled;
For light, and flowers, and gems, and fairest raiment
Were part of that sweet sunshine round her shed:
And nothing to that pure and selfless eye,
But that she loved so well all lovely things:
'Twas love, and love that knew no vanity,
That clothed her bounteous hand with golden rings.

Each circlet was to her some tender token
Of love and friendship, ever deep and dear,—
All sweet and silent pledges still unbroken,
The heart's fond record of each passing year!

Though they might speak of ornament alone
To those who knew not of their gentler part,
The golden token on the finger shone,
The living love was treasured in the heart.

Ah no ! they were no worldly vanities,
More than those fading flowers, these rings of gold ;
But partly like the sweet humanities
That symbolised the simple faiths of old,
In which the mind found many an emblem fair
Of living truths to meet its wild emotions,
And everything in water, earth, and air,
Held sacred in its fanciful devotions.
To her they were the symbols simply wrought,
Of kind remembrance crowned by sweet home-love,
That weakened not the life of holier thought,
That faith in which 'twas hers to live and move.
For Beauty is beloved in every form
And combination where it meets the eye !
Where is the eye that sees no sacred charm
In simple things through love's idolatry?

Within one little golden crypt lies hidden
The sacred hair that graced an honoured head,
O'er which the tear has ofttimes flowed unbidden,
When memory passed its vigil with the dead.

The sweet devotion of a joyous band
Of silver-voicèd maidens all is here,
The dearer still that on this pale cold hand
The gems have sisters now in many a tear.

The fair memorial of some vanished friend,
The little relic of some sweet old day,
Whose memories lie in sunbeams still retained,
Like leaves from dear old summers long away.
And here the bond of true love cherished early,
And nursed in Hope's fair arms the simple tie,
To him whose lone heart now does weep so sorely,
That no sweet tear can cool his fevered eye.

Oh happy, happy days, and tender hours,
When Love was young and Hope in its bright
    morning,
When sunny skies shone o'er a path of flowers,
And some new joy disclosed at every turning.
For through her spirit shone a purer ray
Than ever lit the vanities of earth,
And though she was the gayest of the gay,
There was no folly mingled with her mirth.

They said of old that blessèd spirits shed
A light behind them like a wake of gold,

A halo resting where their wings were spread.
So might the tale of her bright life be told;
For fair as day the path that she has trod ;
With love of friends, with blessings of the poor,
The widow's prayer, the things that live for God,
Her ways were lovely as her faith was sure.
And she is gone ! This day so beautiful,
When like a sun-ray on a woodland stream,
She threw a pleasant light upon us all,
As moves the branches to the water's gleam.

The songs of gladness from her lips were falling,
Like music haunting some still dream of bliss—
The songs of childhood's happy time recalling,
Many an hour of bygone happiness.
And all of us with throbbing hearts did listen :
Ah, never more to hear the songs she sung !
Now other tears upon our eyelids glisten,
Than these sweet tributes to her angel-tongue.
She sung—the accents swelling, trembling, dying—
A simple lay, but with such wondrous fire,
It seemed as if the spirit, heavenward flying,
Had heard the Seraphim's eternal lyre,—
Had heard and drunk with such a rapturous heart
The awful joy of that celestial strain,

With such a longing for an angel's part,
As earthly love might never still again.
Ah me ! and as she sang, the word half spoken,
Was hushed amid that memorable lay :
Her spirit passed as the harp-strings are broken,
Before the last sweet tones have died away.

THE BRAVE OLD LAND.

A VOLUNTEER SONG OF 1860.

WE'LL have no shams among us;
Our work is good and true,
To make the land as strong as
Stout heart and hand can do:
Through all the ages glorious, o'er all the nations grand,
Her ancient days of honour
Shed down their rays upon her;
We'll keep what they have won her,
The Brave Old Land.

She sitteth in her splendour,
　'Mid the thunders of the sea,
Our mother, brave and tender,
　And her faithful sons are we.
We'll give, to guard her sacred shore, our strength of
　heart and hand;
　　And give it as we may, boys,
　　'Tis only half to pay, boys,
　　The debt we owe this day, boys,
　　　The Brave Old Land.

Whatever foes assail her,
　She knows her sons are true;
Their faith will never fail her
　Should friends be far and few.
Our sacred Lady on the throne, amidst her high com-
　mand,
　　We'll circle like a wall,
　　And no danger can befall
　　In the heart of hearts of all
　　　In the Brave Old Land.

The bravest and the best land
  That foot of man hath trod !
The exiles' place of rest, and
  Sweet Liberty's abode !
The gallant hearts who guard so well the flag in her
  right hand,
    For them the page of glory ;
    For us, to ages hoary,
    To keep unstained her story,
      The Brave Old Land.

THE BATTLE OF GILBOA.

THE armies of Achish are pouring from Gath,
From Gaza, and Askelon, low by the shore;
And the people are crushed in their wine-press of
    wrath:
There is ruin behind them and terror before.

Their triumph the cities of Benjamin fills,
From Dan to Beersheba in sackcloth is clad;
Even Judah and Simeon weep on their hills,   ·
Like the Ammonite valleys of Reuben and Gad.

And strong in his sorrows, the worst and the last,
Stands the mighty King Saul, like a rock of the
    flood,
Towering o'er the dark surge of the host heaving past,
With the storm on his breast ever breaking in blood.

All in vain rides young Jonathan, bravest and best,—
  In the fore-front of death rides the loved of the
    land;
All in vain o'er the foe gleams the war-battered crest
  Of great Abner, who fights at his master's right
    hand.

And the battle rolls on, ever redder each wave
  Falling broken, in blood, from the sword of the
    King;
But the hand is withheld that is mighty to save,
  And still closes the foe in a ruddier ring.

In his woe, God-forsaken, and hopeless his host,
  In the day of the Lord, when His judgments befell,
He had wept o'er the grave where his hope lay all lost,
  With the Ancient of Ramah who loved him so well.

He had called forth the visions of death from the
    tomb,
  When his bold heart grew faithless, and feeble his
    sword;
But his legions reel back in the shadow of doom;
  For the Urim is still in the Ark of the Lord.

And the battle rolls on, and the battle rolls on,
  Where the vineyards of Jezreel lie crushed in their
    pride ;
Where the streams of Gilboa are black in the sun,
  And the blood-fringe of Jordan runs red at its side.

And as hopeless as fearless, his crown on his brow,
  With his host scattered far o'er the war-stricken
    field,
Stands the wounded old King, with his face to the foe,
  And their spears falling thick on the boss of his
    shield.

No longer he hears the brave Jonathan's call,
  In the death-front beholds not the plume that he
    wore ;
Ah ! the bravest, the best, the beloved one of all,
  He will scatter the foe on Rock Rimmon no more !

Anon, and great Abner, all reeking and red,
  With his saddle-girths dripping, and death in each
    spring,
Rushes down on the foe, cleaving dead upon dead,
  Through the iron-clad phalanx that closed on the
    King.

And the battle rolls on, and the battle rolls on,
  Through the blood-mist that hangs o'er the war-
      trodden plain,
O'er the merciless riot of slaughter, where none
  Hath a thought for the living, a care for the slain.

" I am wounded full sore," said the King where he lay,
  " But not yet unto death; and the heathen is nigh:
Press thy sword through my breast, since my sons are
      away,
  Ere the heathen behold God's anointed one die."

In the silence of death, in the shadow of night,
  Has their glory gone down through the woe of the
      land ;
In the doom that has broken the sword of their might,
  In the pride of their days, and the strength of their
      hand.

Their swords lay all broken, their bows were all
      strung,
  Where they lay, in their love, round the kingly old
      man ;
And their arms in the house of Ashtaroth were hung,
  And their bones laid to bleach on the walls of
      Beth-shan.

THE WIDOWED SWORD.

ON A FRIEND.

THEY have sent him the sword that his brave boy
wore
   In the field of his young renown,
In the last red field where his faith was sealed,
   And the sun of his days went down.
      Though sad are the tears
        That are blinding him so,
      There is joy in the years
        Of the young head that's low.
And the priceless thing of his father's store
Is the sword that his Brave Boy wore.

'Twas for freedom and home that he gave him away
   Like the sons of his race of old;
And the tears that his father has shed this day
   Make him dearer a thousand-fold.
      There's a glory above him
        To hallow his name;
      A land that will love him,
        Who died for its fame;
And a solace will come when the old heart is sore,
From the sword that his Brave Boy wore.

All so noble, so true, how they stood, how they fell,
   In the battle, the plague, and the cold;
Oh, as bravely and well, as e'er story could tell
   Of the flower of the heroes of old.
      Like a sword through the foe
        Was that fearful attack,
      That so bright ere the blow,
        Comes so bloodily back:
And foremost among them his colours he bore,
And here is the sword that the Brave Boy wore.

And his old father murmurs : The brave are the kind;
   It is more than the Indies to me ;
It tells me how kind and how steadfast of mind
   The soldier to sorrow can be.
       They know well how lonely,
        How grievously wrung,
       Is the heart that its only
        Love loses so young :
And they closed his dark eyes when the battle was
   o'er,
And sent his old father the sword that he wore.

I LOVE BUT THEE ALONE.

No distance ever altered me,
　No time my heart can move,
No beauty win one thought from thee,
　My early, only love.
And though I want the way to woo
　In fancy's flattering tone,
Yet I can tell I love thee well,
　And love but thee alone :
　　Alone, alone, alone—
And love but thee alone.

I love the best, the gentlest grace,
　'Then dearly art thou loved ;
The fairest form, the loveliest face,
　The heart most truly proved ;
But then were I to call them thine,
　Thy blushes would disown,

Though such thou art, as in my heart
   I love but thee alone.
      Alone, alone, alone—
   I love but thee alone.

Of lovelier flowers let others speak,
   That bloom 'neath lovelier skies ;
I know no blossom like thy cheek,
   No sunshine like thine eyes.
And distance ne'er can alter me,
   Nor time, when years are flown ;
One change shall know I love thee so,
   And love but thee alone.
      Alone of all the world—
   Oh, I love but thee alone !

BONAILLIE.

BONAILLIE, O Bonaillie !
  My heart is in this cup o' wine,
And baith I pledge as leal-lie
    As luve can mak' me thine.
      The bugles blaw,
      We maun awa,
The foremost rank is through the Green.
    Bonaillie, O Bonaillie !
Adieu, dear heart o' Aberdeen !

Bonaillie, O Bonaillie !
  The frien'ly grasp my brethren gie ;
But nichtly, luve, and daily,
    My heart maun bide with thee.
      An' never may
      I live the day
I luve thee less, my northern queen.
    Bonaillie, O Bonaillie !
Adieu, dear heart o' Aberdeen !

Bonaillie, O Bonaillie !
  To ane an' a' in this braif toon,
To Provost and to Bailie,
  An' a' the Cooncil roon';
     I'll drink to a',
     Baith great an' sma',
The blithest folk that I hae seen :
    Bonaillie, O Bonaillie !
Adieu, dear heart o' Aberdeen !

Bonaillie, O Bonaillie !
  Gaird-weel the yetts when we're awa ;
An' till we meet again as gaily,
  Oh ! leeze me on ye a'.
     But as for you,
     My ain white doo,
The very apple o' my eyne,
    A thousan' times Bonaillie !
Adieu, dear heart o' Aberdeen !*

  * From "The Midnicht Meeting," a local poem printed for private circulation.

THE WELL OF ARIN.

Far in the North is shining
One star of steady light,
　　That little dreams
　　How dear its beams
Are held by distant things;
What loveless spots are pining
For its beauty all the night;
What bliss about the moorland streams
Its random radiance flings.
How blest it makes one lovely
Forest well, whose crystal eye
Never greets the Sun, and only
That one Star in all the sky!
'Tis the Well of shady Arin
Where the silent waters pour—
The Well that holds the Star in
Its depths for Evermore.

It dreams of it for ever
In the forest's shady gloom,

And all day long
In mournful song
It sings of starry night.
The flowers may fade and never
Shed around their blush of bloom,
And all its summer boughs among
No birds can bring delight.
Its dream of crystal gladness
Is that one sweet random ray;
Its hope of hopeless sadness,
Its love so far away!
And it fills the Well of Arin
With a wine like golden ore—
The Well that holds the Star in
Its depths for Evermore.

A gem upon its bosom,
Through the winter of the year—
A dream of love
Too soon to prove
The poison-sweets of grief.
What cares it for the blossom
That the bright-eyed summers wear,
Though love that looks so far above
Has bliss as sadly brief?
The Star is clothed in glory,

And the Fountain poor and low;
But love has many a story
That the loved one cannot know.
And the woods of shady Arin
Are gathering o'er and o'er
The Well that holds the Star in
Its depths for Evermore.

I know that silver fountain,
And I know that silvan shade—
    I know the low
    And lonely flow
Of song that greets the night.
But it leaves its native mountain
As its sickly fancies fade,
And rolls in gold beneath the glow
Of all the mid-day light.
Its waters as they wander,
Grow all glorious anon,
Till they broaden to the grandeur
Of the beautiful Garonne !
And it is the Well of Arin
Where the sunless waters pour—
The Well that holds the Star in
Its depths for Evermore.

ANNO 1684.

Our Father leads
Us everywhere;
As tenderly He tends our needs
As He upheld with loving care
   The Hebrew child among the reeds;
     Or in the land
     Of Babylon,
Amid the fires, the faithful band,
Who knew Whose strength they rested on
   While in their Father's Hand.

   Though dark our day
   And drear our night,
Though nameless dangers crowd our way,
We know the path that leads us right,
   We know the Guide who cannot stray;
     Though all the land
     Be filled with woe,
And countless foes before us stand,
We know 'tis well, where'er we go,
   When in our Father's Hand.

Q

Whate'er befall,
In bliss or pain,
In doubt or dread, on Him we call;
The Tempter's guile will tempt in vain;
Our Father's Hand is over all.
Though weak we stand,
And lone, and poor,
Or dwell within a bounteous land,
Our path is safe, our place is sure,
When in our Father's Hand.

For all is well
That comes from Him,
And all is true that He doth tell;
The Earth may change, the Sun wax dim,
But change with Him can never dwell!
Nor His command
The worlds gainsay,
Whose path of splendour He hath planned;
And we are sure and safe as they
When in our Father's Hand.

PRINTED BY WILLIAM BLACKWOOD AND SONS, EDINBURGH.

Lately published, by the same Author,

THE MARTYRDOM OF KELAVANE:

A POEM.

Fcap. 8vo, price 2s. 6d.

———

London : Messrs HALL, VIRTUE, AND Co.
Aberdeen : Messrs BROWN AND Co.

———◆———

OPINIONS OF THE PRESS.

The Spectator.

This story is told with spirit and feeling.

The Literary Gazette.

The author of 'The Martyrdom of Kelavane' has been happy in the selection of a subject. Although his treatment of it is by no means equable throughout, he has produced a poem which shows felicity of expression and force of imagination. An excellent action is of primary importance to the poem, although in the present day it is too frequently ignored altogether. Such has not been the case in the present instance. . . . The outline of the story has been filled up by the author with much beauty and pathos, and with a due attention to the facts of history. The continuity of the tale is perhaps broken, and its effect somewhat injured, by the use of a variety of metres in the different sections of the poem. In none of these, however, does the author fail; but over one or two he shows a mastery so complete as to lead us to wish he had confined himself to them.

The Inverness Courier.

This is a touching tale, feelingly told, chaste in style, and conveying a lofty Christian moral. We have to thank the accomplished author for having added so interesting and instructive a volume to our Christian literature.

The Aberdeen Herald.

'Kelavane' is marked more by sweetness, grace, and tenderness, than by any ambitious display of great strength. The nature of the story makes this necessary. Yet there are many passages which exhibit a power, although not higher, yet quite separate from that displayed and required by the present work. For example, we have in one book an argument on Christianity as against mere Deism, of the highest order of philosophical thought, and yet of the most poetical diction. This has seldom been attempted so successfully. Everybody knows how Pope failed. Wordsworth and Coleridge have eminently succeeded, but, saving these masters, there are few beside.

.   .   .   .   .

There are other unconscious displays of peculiar power in different departments of the field of poetry found cropping out here and there throughout this work; but the author himself is plainly steadfast to his purpose to tell the story in all its simple mournfulness.

The Free Press.

A remarkable example of minute, distinctive, and graphic portraiture is that of the Arabian mare. Mr Forsyth has studied the points of a hunter to good purpose. The competent reader will not question his title

> "To paint
> Her picture for a monument."

> A coal-black maré without a speck,
> Save on her brow one starry fleck ;
> Her race was of the wingèd feet,
> Of silken Sholakla the fleet.
> Her head was thin, her nostrils wide,
> Her dark eyes flashed with fiery pride,
> Yet soft and liquid not the less
> To tell her native gentleness.
> Her chest was broad, her shoulders free,
> For swiftness and for symmetry ;
> Her gleaming neck with streaming main,
> So noble all her fine fore-train
> Rose straight as maiden's from her breast,
> And like a swan's her curving crest,
> With watchful ears erect and small,
> That knew her master's softest call ;
> With stately gait and easy grace,
> A face that looked man in the face.
> Her back was straight, her limbs were long,
> With instep high and pasterns strong,
> In small round hooves like pillars set,
> As hard as steel, as black as jet.
> The Alpine he-goat's foot had she,
> The household dog's docility ;
> The beauty of the Arab breed,
> The courage of the Tartar steed,
> And like a banner in the gale
> Far streamed behind her silken tail."

The Presbyterian Messenger.

A touching story exquisitely told ; a poem of a very high order, rich with imagination and glowing with beauty, descriptive of a character of natural grandeur and superiority, still more grand for her firm adherence to her faith, and more simple by her earnest childlike trust in Christ, ennobled by her exalted conception of Christianity.